A TIMELESS PASSION

A TIMELESS PASSION

NAIM ATTALLAH

QUARTET BOOKS

First published in Great Britain in 1995 by
Quartet Books Ltd
A member of the Namara Group
27 Goodge Street
London W1P 1FD

Copyright © Naim Attallah 1995

All rights reserved. No part of this book may
be reproduced in any form or by any means without
the prior written permission of the publisher

A catalogue record for this title is available
from the British Library

ISBN 0 7043 7098 0

Phototypeset by Intype, London
Printed and bound in Great Britain by
WBC Bookbinders, Bridgend, Mid Glamorgan

Acknowledgement

I should like to pay tribute to my editor Jennie Bradshaw, who has worked closely with me for many years. Her contribution to this first novel has been invaluable.

For Maria
who never wavers

One

Carlo surveys the land of his birth and contemplates death. He has come a long way and has a long way still to go. He is more used to airports and fast cars than to railway stations, but for this last sentimental journey he has taken a flight only as far as Rome. For the final few hundred miles he has chosen to travel by train. For one thing it will give him time.

Time is something he feels he needs but does not understand. How can it be that now and then time appears to move slowly, even to the point of standing still? Does the drowning man really see his life paraded before him? Quite possibly, Carlo thinks, feeling his throat tighten on the nodule of grief. Since the news of his mother's death, less than twenty-four hours before, something has happened to upset the balance of time.

As he gazes out of the carriage window it is difficult for him to believe that so definite and divisible an element as time can move at different rates. He tries to grasp the enormity of bereavement. And as he does so the gentle rhythms of the train together with the toilsome workings of his mind persuade him that this moment in his life and what might be called real time are utterly distinct from each other.

His mother's death has struck at the very core of his being. It is not that it was untimely or unnatural or even unexpected (she was very frail). It is the finality he cannot accept, the removal of his cornerstone and the assault on his senses. He is almost sixty years of age, the dynamic head of a large advertising agency, highly regarded, and with all the trappings of wealth and success. He is certainly old enough and sufficiently robust to take the death of a parent in his stride. He is therefore both ashamed and dismayed by the intensity of his feelings.

Everything is happening either very slowly, or very quickly; he is not sure which. The Italian countryside flashes by in a patchwork of vineyards and olive trees, haphazardly stitched together by threads of orange blossom. And the pale blue hills decorated with black cypress stripes threaten to encroach on the grey landscape of his mind, disfigured by grief.

★ ★ ★

Fifty years before, an eight year old boy is standing on tiptoe peering into an open wooden box where his father lies dead. He holds his mother's hand which is soft with sorrow. He is told to say goodbye. The room is filled with people he knows mostly from family albums, a cortège of photos now made flesh. Will Papa hear his farewell, feel the kiss upon his cold cheek? He is not sure. He is present at an adult ritual, an uncertain guest in a private domain. He knows instinctively that he is living the moment of greatest significance in his whole life, the moment when time stands still before marking the end of something beautiful.

He feels very little, only a dull ache in his stomach which on any other day might be mistaken for hunger. He is unacquainted with grief. He tries to force his mind round the thought that he will never again talk with, laugh with, roll on the ground with his father, his wonderfully English father. But he cannot summon the emotions to match the immensity of the loss. In Italy tears are not proscribed. Even so he cannot cry.

All eyes are on him as he bids farewell. A son and his father: the ultimate valediction. Or so it seems to the onlookers, voyeurs at an intimate rite of passage: boy becoming man. There are muted exchanges above his head, flashes of brave smiles, gestures of chagrin and discomfort. Words like 'serene' and 'peaceful' hang in the air like beads of bereavement. Rituals are for grown-ups; they make pain tolerable.

'Be brave,' says his Neapolitan uncle, weeping openly and running his rough country fingers through Carlo's hair. But there is no need for Carlo to feel brave. The freshness of youth blunts the spearhead of desolation and prevents his heart from breaking. He feels a certain pang, but he experiences it not as pain, but as another and different form of pleasure, not unlike the first inchoate stirrings of sexual desire. The sadness is to come later, obliquely and often indistinctly. For the moment he is spared its keenness.

★ ★ ★

Carlo has an imperfect memory of his father's death, now blurred by the passage of time and the faithlessness of oral history. Even the image of his father in a coffin, graven on his heart, is now vague and ill-defined in his mind. But he still recalls the difficulty he experienced in knowing how to grieve, the effort involved in striking an attitude of sadness, made worse by the fact that it was so clearly expected of him. In the scheme of things his father's untimely death was much worse: without purpose, against all known and accepted laws of nature, a man cut down in his prime. How then to explain the searing intensity of his feelings now? He cannot account for the degree of wretchedness he feels.

How beautiful are the colours of southern Italy. The railway cuts through the broad valley clothed in yellow-green clover. Here and there the river glints silver in the afternoon sun. The surrounding slopes are topped with rust-red monasteries. All around there is evidence of a lifestyle which has vanished elsewhere: men leaning on sickles, muleteers watering their animals, old women clothed in black, water-pots on their heads, wending their way up mountain tracks. The landscape is heavy with time, the weight of the past straining the present.

Carlo is much given to introspection, though he considers it dangerous. He is doubtful of its benefits, believing that prolonged self-analysis merely sharpens the tools of further introspection. And that, he fears, could lead ultimately to self-destruction. He once contemplated therapy but immediately rejected the idea. He despises therapists and all those associated with the tawdry commercial aspects of other people's soul baring. Counselling, that modern marvel, is on offer everywhere, even in Carlo's own advertising company whose executives are thought to be particularly susceptible to the stresses of modern life in the metropolis. Therapy is meant to cure everything from childhood abuse to premature ejaculation. The absurdity of the idea angers him.

Carlo himself would be perfect material for the analyst. His dual nationality entails a divided personality most obvious in the eternal dichotomy between his head and his heart. He craves the Englishness of his father, the distant hero. Carlo's whole adult life has been an attempt at emulation: his defection to London, his marriage abroad, the rending of roots, the recanting of his childhood faith. And for what? To be like a man he hardly knew and scarcely remembered.

Because his father has been dead for so long, Carlo finds he can make him into anything he likes. And he does. In his mind his father has become urbane, charming, self-possessed, unexcitable, quintessentially English. He is the antithesis of the hot-blooded Latin, the predominant role model for young Italian boys. His father is rendered romantic by remoteness. Carlo longs to be like him, even to *be* him in some inscrutable fantastic way. In this endeavour he has enjoyed a measure of success. But the tension remains. And the dichotomy is one he prefers to resolve by himself, to share with no one, not even his wife. His dear sweet Flora. His English rose.

★ ★ ★

They lie in bed, their bodies not quite touching, energies gentled by two decades of marriage.

— *Perhaps we should have a cuddle if you're going to be away for a whole week.*

Genteel. Refined. Considerate.

— *After all, funerals are never easy, especially if it's family.*

Sensible. Sober. Controlled.

— *You know, I'd come with you if you thought it would help.*

Caring. Composed. Supportive.

She climbs on top of him, remembering that she had lain underneath last time.

Methodical.

— *But it's the worst time of year for me to get away, what with the children's exams and the new conservatory and the garden . . .*

Prudent. Pragmatic. Efficient.

With deft accomplished strokes she stimulates an erection.

Talented.

— I'm sure your relatives will be a great source of strength. It's such a long time since you've seen them all.

Imaginative. Sympathetic.

— I will miss you, you know. We all will.

Sweet. Affectionate.

She caresses his cock and guides it home.

Tender.

— I'm going to try and lose weight while you're away.

Resolute. Optimistic.

She sighs contentedly and engages in the familiar rhythms.

— Darling, I do love you.

Devoted.

They finish what they have begun. More for comfort than for passion.

* * *

The train pulls out of the last important town before his destination. A flutter of nuns scurry off the platform, eager for the sanctuary of the cloisters. The dark-apricot houses sit more closely together than Carlo remembers, but otherwise everything seems remarkably unchanged. Mattresses dangle over the iron grilles of cluttered balconies, and washing hangs frivolously next to churches. The louvred wooden shutters remain closed and hold the day in suspension.

Death challenges the living. It is an intimation of our own mortality. All the clichés are true. A major part of Carlo's life has just fallen away. It is much more than a replaceable segment; it is elemental and vital to the whole balance of his existence.

Carlo feels doubly challenged. He has long since turned his back on his origins to explore what he feels to be his destiny. He does not feel treacherous because there has been no betrayal involved. His early days have not been desecrated; they remain enshrined in rose-coloured wadding. For the first time he understands that the life he has embraced is possible only because of his mother. So long as his mother lived, the childlike idyll and the chosen path of the grown man were held in beautiful equilibrium. His mother was the link between his past and his present.

Though he lives in self-imposed exile, she did not forsake him, nor he her. Because she married his father there was a corner of her own heart which belonged forever to England. And because she was Carlo's mother she understood what he yearned for. She stoked the fires of his dreams.

Yet he needs her to live out the dream. Without her everything hangs in the balance, the edifice will crumble. His life will become a sham, unsustainable. He trembles at the thought.

The train slows as it approaches the station, and he glimpses the sombre faces of his brothers waiting to meet him. His head fills with memories of paradise lost, and his heart groans with the weight of days long gone. *His sentence is passed.*

Two

Sometimes there is no need to see people's faces to know they are sad. You can tell even from the backs of their heads that they have tears in their eyes. Carlo senses all this as he walks in silence behind his two brothers, and instinctively takes on their sorrowful shuffling gait. One brother carries Carlo's suede leather bag, the other the large wreath of arum lilies he bought at Leonardo da Vinci airport. Carlo carries nothing save his thoughts.

Medieval towns have a timeless quality. The life within them may change over the years, but the architecture is so prominent, the style so unmistakable that somehow a sense of the immortal is superimposed. Carlo is grateful for this. It makes his home-coming bearable.

The ancient archways, the narrow fishbone streets, the cobbled stairways, the small shops all tug at the secret places of his memory. Through a dozen doorways he sees old women in bunchy black skirts and knitted shawls busying themselves with the last tasks of the day. Others have completed the day's work and sit outside with their menfolk on gnarled wooden benches. There are toothless gums, twisted limbs and faces etched with hardship and happiness.

As he climbs the three whitewashed steps into his childhood home, a young woman calls to another from the balcony above. Her cry echoes the silent scream inside him.

★ ★ ★

Few deaths are capable of touching us deeply; perhaps only two or three in a lifetime, no more. Where his heart should be there is a gaping hole. Can one *feel* a hole? At this moment Carlo imagines he can. He is suddenly overcome by a weariness which grants him an illusory peace.

He expects her to be in her bedroom. He is therefore taken aback at the sight of the coffin when he pushes open the door of the family room downstairs. It lies on the solid wooden table, which is bleached from generations of vigorous scrubbing. It is the table where they all sat as children breaking bread and relishing the flavours of crushed fennel and fresh herbs. His first reaction is to wonder where people will eat now the table is thus occupied, but he immediately dismisses the thought as trivial and unworthy. Respect for the dead is burned into the brain of every convent child.

There is now no trace of cooking smells. Instead the air hangs heavy with incense and the sweetish odour of decay. The shutters are closed, but they cannot completely stave off the stifling heat. Only the stone floor feels cool.

Everything is as it should be in accordance with Catholic ritual. The body is decently laid out; candles burn on either side; the hands are folded upon the breast in the form of a cross. A bottle of holy water sits on a nearby shelf next to a statue of the Madonna bedecked in rosary beads. The coffin itself is unexpectedly elaborate, nothing too ornate, but enough to show that a concern with appearances and reputations is universal.

Suddenly the door closes from the other side. He is quite alone with his dead mother. He fixes his gaze on the corpse, unexpectedly life-like. The purple veins stand proud on her hands, like the rivers on a map. The loose skin lies in folds round her once beautiful neck. Guardian of a thousand secrets, comforter in time of need, faithful defender. He tries to submit himself to the metaphysics of memory, but the ordinary objects in the room intervene. He finds these the most poignant: the unfinished sewing, the dainty summer shoes, the half-read book. They enter his soul and overlay his grief.

When I was a child, I spake as a child, I understood as a child, I thought as a child: but when I became a man, I put away childish things. Through a glass darkly he surveys his past, and knows for the first time he is a child no longer.

★ ★ ★

The cold tap produces a stream of peat-brown water. He lies back in the bathtub and enjoys the semi-darkness of the shuttered room. He washes away the grime of his journey and the dust of nostalgia. Thus far he has not lost his composure. The main thing is to stay in control, not to yield to the ghosts of the past.

What he most fears is that the English *sang-froid* he has worked so hard at cultivating over the years will desert him just when he needs it most. He has nothing to put in its place, certainly nothing as beautifully detached as English phlegm. He does not even have the rod of religion any longer. As a Roman Catholic he has long since lapsed.

Why is it that only Catholics 'lapse'? One never hears of lapsed Presbyterians, or lapsed Zen Buddhists for that matter. There must be a reason, but for the moment he cannot think of one. It was not the standard crisis of faith – the prerogative of convent-educated people – which led him into a doctrinal wilderness. Indeed the thought of leaving his faith behind along with his country never occurred to him. His experience was more like that of Orpheus who, glancing back at his beloved

Eurydice, saw her vanish into the shades to be lost to him forever.

As a boy, however, he had always felt rather pleased and privileged to be taught by nuns. In those days it was a concession granted to fatherless sons. The convent was on the edge of town (unlike the monastery which was several miles away up a dusty track on the hillside) which meant that he and his brothers could go home to their mother at night after vespers.

The rule of enclosure was lifted in the nineteenth century, and since that time the sisters of Santa Scholastica had turned their goodness outwards and welcomed the faithful into their midst. They followed the tenets of St Benedict, the twin brother of their founder, and were devoted to learning and good works. The Rule of St Benedict lays stress on a way of life in which chastity and poverty are dominant factors, but this did not stop the sisters sharing what little they had with those who entered their convent. Indeed the inscription above the door read: 'Let all guests who arrive be received like Christ. And to all let due honour be shown.'

At the heart of their conviction was the idea

that through prayer they could change the world. It was a principle which they tried hard to impart to those in their charge. Carlo's days were therefore marked out in prayers: prayers of adoration, thanksgiving, petition and contrition; prayers for the dead, prayers for the living, prayers for all the miserable sinners.

★ ★ ★

The convent is a place of sensual pleasures: the swish of starched black habits, the comforting click of rosary beads, the rich aromas of beeswax and incense. They are part of the sedative, seductive power of religion. They stroke the senses and warm the spirit.

The boy feels safe here. He submits to a wisdom far greater than his own. His life is filled with simple certainties, fixed truths. The Catechism is learned by heart, the responses are inbred. In the morning the nuns greet him with a Benedicamus Domino, and he smiles a Deo gratias in return.

The convent is also a place of mystery, of improbable happenings: faith emanating from doubt, light from darkness. The boy is quite untroubled by these paradoxes.

He places complete trust in the sisters though he knows that they too are living contradictions. They are women of quite remarkable strength and spirit and self-possession, yet they teach the children to be docile, obedient and passive.

The sisters' lives are predicated on being virgins, yet there are constant dark references to forbidden fruits. Everyone is in a state of sin, everyone is carnal, and there is something called concupiscence which is shrouded in secrecy. Little children try to grapple with the enormity of evil, and after a while guilt is as natural as breathing.

The boy's day is shaped by Hail Marys and Angelus bells, by holy pictures and gold-leaf breviaries. These are the divine trimmings of his faith. On Feast Days he lays lilies at the feet of the Virgin's statue. At First Communion he is intoxicated by the beauty of the young brides in their white dresses, transported by the purity of their tulle veils under garlands of flowers. None of this is registered consciously. But everything is imprinted.

In the library which is used as a classroom there hangs on the wall a picture of Jesus on the Cross. His eyes are closed, signifying death. The children are told by Sister Ignatia that if they look long enough they will see Jesus's eyes open again. 'His passion overcomes death. Because of Him the dead shall live again.'

Carlo stares at Jesus's eyes till his own eyes hurt. But Sister Ignatia is right. The painting speaks the truth. Life comes from death. If you look long enough, if you believe hard enough, Jesus's eyes open. He is alive.

He wishes he had known how to make this happen when his father's eyes closed for the last time.

* * *

The evening sun is sinking behind the hills in the distance like a magnificent copper pot nestling on the hob. Carlo has changed into clean clothes and is heading for the family church. He picks his way through the familiar network of alleys and passages linking the intimate assortment of painted medieval houses.

The Chiesa della Madonna del Rosario is a modest church whose façade gives on to the little piazza encircled by pink and white oleanders. It is flanked by two *campanili* square towers crowned with a single arch on each side. Like all Italian churches its door is open, promising sanctuary from the outside world.

He feels that he has stopped behaving rationally

and is falling back on his instincts. He is conscious of a need to be gentle with himself. He also feels that certain things have to be done, certain solemn rites have to be observed. One of these is to go to the family church and light a candle for his dead mother.

He does not dare to examine this impulse too closely; he knows that it will not bear scrutiny. He is used to making considered judgements, careful decisions; he thinks they put a finer grid on life. The daily task he sets himself, both in the business world and in his private life, is daunting: it is to behave intelligently (and thus, he believes, morally). This involves examining his own motives, as well as other people's, analysing statements, weighing arguments. He tries never to act recklessly.

Men in general impute the highest motives to everything they undertake; and Carlo is no exception in this. He wants to impose sense on the chaos of day to day living, believing moreover that it is a worthy business to engage in. He is keen to understand the world and to make it an ordered place.

There is however a tension between believing

something to be profoundly true, to the point of actually *feeling* it, and in that sense knowing it to be true; and particular behaviour which cannot be reconciled with that conviction. His intellect tells him that to go to church when he is no longer one of the faithful borders on hypocrisy and perfidy. But his intellect is suffused with the most intense emotion. As he pushes open the heavy wooden door leading into the nave of the Madonna del Rosario, Carlo feels the *pull* of religion.

★ ★ ★

He waits for his eyes to adjust to the gloom. The only light comes from a few dozen candles guttering on a piece of rough hewn wood in the left transept. There are fourteen stained glass windows, seven on each side of the nave, but the sun is now too weak to filter through them. Beneath each window is a wooden carving depicting a Station of the Cross, and by extension the suffering of humanity.

He knows the church intimately, though it is as

if he is seeing it for the first time. He moves haltingly up the aisle, fingering the hard oak of the pews like a blind man feeling his way. He approaches the wooden crucifix suspended from the faded stuccoed ceiling. Christ is draped round the Cross in a contortion of wretchedness; his body is twisted and knotted above the smooth carved letters: *Ego sum via, veritas, lux*. It is a triumph of art and divinity that in this comfortless picture the agony of the body is sublimated in a holiness of spirit.

A gentle genuflection – a conditioned response, a symbolic endorsement of his past. He looks round to see if he has been observed, but he is quite alone. With a sense of relief he slumps on the steps of the altar and looks around him.

High above on the ceiling the frescoes feature a profusion of cherubim and archangels, emmisaries from heaven. Lack of realism is offset by a bounty of symbolism. The effect is rather like waking up in the middle of a child's lavishly illustrated storybook. Art and artefacts are exalted by a sense of continuity, a timelessness.

Behind the candles in the transept is the familiar fresco of the *Mater Dolorosa* which Carlo has known since boyhood. She is depicted with the utmost simplicity, which is the supreme strength of the painting. There are no fine clothes, no jewels, no adornments to detract from her purity. Carlo feels her presence and considers her anew.

Mother and Virgin: a sublime contradiction. She is slender, pale, delicate, wistful, above all gentle. She presides over a mystery which is removed from any recognizable reality, and yet she stirs men and women all over the world to the noblest emotions. She fills them with love and pity and awe, and her mystery endures.

Carlo contemplates the painting and is deeply moved. Its beauty holds the tension between sorrow and joy in exquisite balance. The Holy Mother weeps, and her tears offer hope and promise. Carlo wonders why tears, unlike any other bodily excretion, are considered to be pure. And now he understands that it is because of the Madonna. Her tears are like purified water, imbued with the properties of life. They can help make her son whole again. Her tears offer solace to the bereaved; she laments with them and shares their sadness. And her grief is not without meaning, for soon it will be transfigured into joy and exultation.

Carlo feels he is at the crossroads where time and eternity meet. He has become aware of something profoundly significant. He cradles his face in his hands. He is a man who has almost forgotten how to weep, but his hurt is so great that the tears flow easily and abundantly.

He looks back at the Madonna. Slowly but unmistakably she steps out of the painting towards him. Through a watery mist he sees her beautiful features picked out in the glimmer of candlelight. He is operating in that tiny space where illusion and reality meet.

He is afraid. His senses are under siege. He attempts to pull himself together. At that moment she takes a taper and lights a candle. Her face is radiant and she smiles towards him. *He has received his cross.*

Three

Sexual desire is anarchic, unpredictable. It strikes unbidden and overwhelms its victim. The signs are unequivocal and are difficult to ignore. All of this Petra is used to. It has happened before on many occasions. But that she should be seized by carnal urges in church, in the presence of the Holy Spirit, is quite exceptional, and more than she can comfortably bear.

She has a system for dealing with such attacks, and she immediately puts it into effect. It is the same principle which governs routine fire drills: to walk calmly away from the source of the flames. But as she strides purposefully out of the Madonna del Rosario, the man with tears in his eyes is following closely behind.

The church was so dimly lit that she had not at first noticed him. She had come to light a candle and have a moment's peace and prayer, but her silence with God was disturbed by a sob, the quiet choking sound of a solitary lament. It was not the weeping and wailing of a miserable sinner come to abase himself before his God; nor the keening of a professional mourner; rather the constrained cry of a man of sorrow, and as such it was beautiful and seductive. She felt it in her sex.

Now he is alongside her.

— *I'm so sorry. I didn't mean to embarrass you . . .*

He is disturbingly attractive. His face is still taut and tense, his dark brown eyes still moist, but he manages a weak smile. Petra has a fondness for fragility, especially in men in whom — in her experience — it is so rare. Indeed she has a fondness for many things which men are usually happy to provide. She is a woman of prodigious appetite, but after twenty dismal years of marriage and self-restraint she has learned to live with disappointment.

— *You see, I thought I was alone . . .*

Like a great many women Petra enjoys sex, but that in itself presents a threat to her husband. He, like a great many men, perceives her enjoyment as a bid for counter-dominance, which makes it unacceptable to his male ego. He does not articulate it to himself in quite this way; he merely regards her as precocious, and that is not a virtue in a wife. Men are often confused about women, particularly in societies whose moral tone is set by a celibate clergy. In Italy virginity and motherhood are still considered the most estimable positions for women. And Petra is neither a virgin nor a mother.

— *My name is Bartlett, by the way. Giancarlo Bartlett.*

Nothing she was taught at school, nothing she learned at her mother's feet prepared her for the searing intensity of desire. Her grandmother had also educated her in the ways of men and imparted invaluable nuggets of wisdom on the subject. But no one had ever tried to convey the awesome power of desire, the way it can suddenly rage through the body like a sandstorm. She feels it now as this beautiful man holds out his graceful hand in greeting.

— *I'm only visiting . . .just here for a few days . . .*

She thinks it might have been different if there had not been such a concentration on purity in her formative years. Purity complicates the sexual response in both men and women. Being constantly exhorted to be chaste often has the perverse effect of encouraging an inordinate interest in sex. This is certainly the way it is with Petra. But she knows she is by no means alone. Indeed she has discovered from her academic research that a large majority of ascetic monks and celibate priests are preoccupied with a struggle against concupiscence. This has serious implications for their vocation.

— *I used to live in the town . . .this is where I grew up in fact . . .*

One problem is that since her marriage offers so little in the way of satisfaction, her sexual feelings have often become quite separated from love. This might have been a difficulty, both for her and her religion, but over the years she has worked out a personal morality which does not offend her own theology. She herself has always thought of sexual congress as the most innocent of activities. She likes to think that God, whom she worships, might also regard it in this light. It pleases her to imagine that it is only a question of time and God's judgement before the link between divine love and sexual love is revealed. But it is a sophisticated notion and God has to wait until his people are ready to receive it.

In the meantime Petra must try to control her desire.

★ ★ ★

Carlo walks back to the family house in a daze. He feels embarrassed and ashamed that he should have allowed himself to fall apart so completely. And in such an undignified manner. He is profoundly disappointed in himself. He must not let it happen again.

The business in church had been mortifying, made worse by the presence of the woman. In retrospect he cannot imagine how she had seemed so perfectly to overlay the image of the Madonna. Of course the light was poor, and he was in some distress, but even so the very idea now strikes him as utterly foolish and absurd. At the time, however, he knows he felt it with the intensity of a religious experience.

He thinks how very surprised his wife would have been to witness his emotional display in the church. And afterwards the awkward, bumbling attempt to apologize and explain to the woman of immaculate appearance. She was quite inscrutable, and reticent to the point of muteness. He had not even ascertained her name. All in all he had conducted himself very clumsily. His wife would certainly have been quite taken aback.

To Carlo's surprise he finds it difficult to bring to mind a picture of his wife. He can hear her voice, but in place of her face there is just a rough outline, like the first faint contour of a portrait sketch. One of her many virtues, he reflects, is the way in which her own impeccable composure injects Carlo's demeanour with a gentle constraint. While she is by his side he is self-possessed, level-headed, imperturbable. He suddenly feels threatened by her absence.

Darkness is falling as he makes his way back to the house. He takes an indirect route, hoping to buy some time and peace of mind. The evening noises, different from those of the day, fill the air. Music and laughter, the weary wailing of babies on the brink of sleep, the clatter from kitchens – all these and a hundred other sounds are magnified by the stone walls and narrow streets. Everywhere there is an energy and vitality from which Carlo feels quite remote and set apart.

His mother's house is also filled with the clatter of normal living. His brothers, their wives and children are all engaged in the natural negotiation of family affairs. Even in death, it seems, life continues unabated. He takes comfort from this thought, but is faintly troubled by its implied indifference.

When any group of people are gathered together, the real test of their love and compassion is the extent to which they open their hearts and welcome someone from the outside. On this analysis Carlo's family fail the test. Or so he thinks. But in truth he does not know any more whether his feeling of being on the outside, of being *excluded*, comes from others, or from the depths of his own anguished soul. With this thought he slumps into the narrow bed of his childhood, easing himself between the sheets like a blind man finding solace in the familiar.

★ ★ ★

Invocations to the Virgin Mary bestow a rhythm on the year. It is the Feast of the Annunciation, a celebration of the day when the Angel Gabriel was sent by God to Nazareth and greeted Mary with the Words 'Hail, full of grace.' The children of the convent, small creatures in black smocks and floppy ties, are preparing for the arrival of the priest to say Mass. Like belfry bats, the sisters of Santa Scholastica flit and fluster in anticipation of a man coming in their midst.

The twelve-year-old boy has a desire to please. He is to serve at the altar for the first time. He is overwhelmed by the gravity of his office, the responsibility of his role. But he rejoices at the prospect. He must not disappoint. The sisters have placed their trust in him, and his beloved mother will attend the Mass.

The sisters prepare the children by carefully explaining the symbolism and significance of the Eucharist, the blood and the body. It is a familiar story, part of the daily diet of the convent. But special tuition is given to the boy who has been chosen to serve. He regards this as a privilege, and feels proud and favoured. He learns that the holy candle represents the divinity of Christ. When he asks why, he is told it is because the bees collect the wax from only the sweetest and most fragrant flowers. As the candle burns it symbolizes the self-immolation of Christ, but its light brightens the path to heaven. The boy is wide-eyed at the wonder and mystery of it all. It is like a glorious fairy-tale told by angels.

He has also been instructed in the allegory of the bell which, as altar boy, he must ring at a given signal from the priest. This will happen twice, at the Sanctus and at the Elevation. He can scarcely contain his excitement. Sister Ignatia's eyes are gentle and benign. She tells her charge that the bell for the Mass is no ordinary bell. It is first washed with blessed water; then it is annointed with chrism, a consecrated oil; and finally it is placed on a thurible with burning incense. The task of the bell-ringer is to excite the attention and devotion of the faithful. It is a very important ritual. The boy gazes devotedly into Sister Ignatia's face, so pure yet so beguiling.

'In nomine Patris, et Filii, et Spiritus Sancti...' The familiar chant heralds the beginning of the Mass. The boy walks behind the priest, a dutiful disciple. He knows the order of service by heart, and even now he recites it inwardly to himself like a solemn mantra. He is filled with a sense of occasion. He must not miss his cue. He looks to Sister Ignatia for reassurance. She wears a solemn smile of unimpeachable chastity. He feels quite weak.

The boy stands at the priest's right hand, servant of God. The air is thick with incense which invades his nostrils, cloyingly. There is something wrong, something unaccountably strange about his surroundings, as if he is stuck in the middle of a jigsaw where the pieces do not quite fit. He is seized by a kind of stagefright. Everything is happening far too quickly. An unstoppable spate of lessons and responses. His eyelids keep closing.

'Sanctus, Sanctus, Sanctus...' The moment has come for him to do his duty. He reaches out for the bell but his hand feels heavy and sluggish. The priest is looking sternly at him. With a supreme effort the boy grasps the bell and rings it vigorously. His skin feels clammy. The sound travels through his body and gives

him a curious tingling sensation. He looks to Sister Ignatia, but her radiance is now eclipsed by an expression of lust and provocation. Everything is going out of control. He feels quite faint. This is not how it is meant to be.

'Hoc est meum corpus . . .' Here is my body. The boy wishes he could leave his own body behind but he is fixed to the spot. The pace is quickening. It is already the Elevation. He reaches for the bell again, but instead his hand is inexorably drawn to the stiffness beneath his cassock. He turns in horror to Sister Ignatia, who beams in approbation. Sins and sanctions surge into his head.

He turns away to hide his mortification. And there behind the altar is the painting of the Mater Dolorosa which does not belong in the convent at all. And beneath the painting on a solid wooden table lies his beautiful mother in a coffin, her shrouded body draped in rosary beads. He cannot understand anything now. He looks imploringly at the Virgin, and the shame which he feels at the swelling in his cassock is gently suffused by mysterious pleasure. The priest starts the Pater Noster and everyone joins in the prayer which Christ taught his disciples. The boy opens his mouth but the words do not come. Instead his hands rub the rhythm of the Christian creed on his blazing body.

Then the worst happens. He knows it is going to happen and he cannot do anything to stop it. The Madonna is suddenly transformed and transfigured into the woman from the church who comes towards him, smiling beatifically, carrying a candle. She cradles it in her hands, then takes it to her bosom, pressing it between her pale pink breasts. She puts it slowly to her face and brushes it with her lips. The candle immediately ignites and warm liquid wax spills down on to her naked body.

Carlo wakes in a stream of shame. *He has fallen.*

Four

Death is the most ordinary of occurrences, but its power to transform the world of the living is formidable. Carlo feels quite debilitated by events. It is not just the bereavement; it is the feelings attendant on bereavement and their ability to turn an ordered existence upside down. He has been here before, that is to say he has sometimes felt challenged by the business of living, the grittiness of everyday problems, and the insidious way they introduce an element of chaos.

Because he is a supremely rational being, he has a favoured way of dealing with complications, which is (after an initial period of agonizing) to take the Hamlet view: *'There is nothing either good or bad, but thinking makes it so.'* This goes against the grain of course, given his propensity for careful thought and self-examination. To decide *not* to think about something is a tacit admission that thinking about it can actually make it worse; whereas his ethical seriousness and belief in the power of reasoning naturally suggest otherwise.

However reluctant he is to admit it, even to himself, he does know that thinking too hard can sometimes land him in trouble. With grief, as with faith, perhaps it might be better simply to accede to its power; though acceding to anything without the utmost consideration strikes Carlo as a perilous path. Faith, he grants, may be an exception. In his more reflective moments he has sometimes thought that the truth of Christianity, if it exists at all, is entirely subjective. It depends entirely on the fact that people engage in the practice of it, which lends it a kind of authority; but objectively speaking it has no truth at all.

Carlo does not regard this as an irreverent thought, far less an iniquitous one; more an idea that belongs to the realm of philosophical abstraction. Could Christianity exist in a kind of vacuum without people practising it? Can any kind of truth have an independent existence, removed from those who believe it? Somehow he thinks not.

Even with something less abstract like a work of art, perhaps it too needs human appraisal to count as good art. And yet this cannot be the whole answer. Supposing a painting is locked away in a cellar hidden from view — the idea is not such a strange one — and the artist has completed his task (he may even be dead), which means that nothing is going to affect the intrinsic merit of the painting. What is done is done, what is art is art; but can it *count* as art if it is locked in the cellar? Somehow it is so difficult to think of artistic worth existing in isolation.

And what bearing does all this have on his grief? Only that grief surely has no validity as an independent entity; it is an elusive state, but it is above all an expression of loss, and entirely dependent on there being a connection between two people. The closer the connection, the greater the grief. These are the sober thoughts which Carlo lays like a pall over the beginnings of the new day.

★ ★ ★

All the major occasions in life – birth, marriage, death – are surrounded by elements of ritual. The form they take may vary from place to place but they are united in their gravity of purpose. There is an instinctive human need to pay homage to those we have loved. This exists even where religion plays no part, although ministry at death remains one of the most self-evidently purposeful tasks of the Church.

As Carlo walks with his brothers behind the coffin, he reflects that the business of honouring the dead is done quite splendidly by the Church. Funerals in southern Italy are scenic affairs, and the formalities for Carlo's mother are no exception. They have all the ingredients of a dramatic spectacle, part pageant, part mystery play. The cortège proceeds at a slow march, the tempo matched by the toll of the bell in the piazza. The coffin is borne high by four young men, their sombre dress contrasting with the bright wreaths of marigolds and lilies. The early June sun beats down from a gentian blue sky and mocks the mourners.

The procession is headed by two priests, both reciting solemnly from their breviaries, and as it moves through the sunlight towards the shadows of the Madonna del Rosario people in the street stop and make the sign of a cross. Old men rise stiffly from their café tables, doffing their crumpled caps, and gossipy groups outside doorways fall silent. For a moment Carlo's private grief seems universal.

Inside the church the coffin is placed in the centre aisle and sprinkled with holy water. '*Requiem aeternam dona eis Domine* . . .Eternal rest grant unto them, O Lord . . .' The opening petition uniting the quick and the dead breaks into the muffle of the mourners, demanding attention. The Requiem Mass is disconcerting in its sure and certain simplicity. There is no pious veneer, only an unchanging conviction given expression in words and actions.

Carlo tries to mix the pain he feels with the ceremonial constants: the music, the liturgy, the accoutrements of worship, the sundry symbols of the life everlasting. Thus far he is in control. There is a cold space underneath his rib cage which is at variance with his body temperature, but he tries desperately to focus on things outside himself. He concentrates on the responses – *Kyrie eleison, Chri-*

ste eleison, Kyrie eleison – and feels the incense dry his throat.

Carlo wonders how many masses for the dead have been said inside this very church; he thinks of those now departed who themselves must have stood here, on this very spot where he is standing, and heard the same words; and he imagines those not yet born who will one day do the same when he himself is gone. The enigma of time, the riddle of death – neither can be wholly understood, but in their timeless liturgical expression, they can be wondered at and extolled.

'*O Lord, deliver the souls of all the faithful departed from the pains of hell . . .and may they not fall into darkness . . .*' The ritual words have a quiet, austere dignity; they are personal and impersonal, they edify and gratify, they express hope and fear, and they transcend both. They seem to Carlo to take place not just inside this church, here and now, but in all churches everywhere and somehow outside of time itself, or at least our imperfect understanding of it. Viewed in this way the church is an ever fixed point of permanence in all the ebb and flow of history. The thought of this soothes and comforts.

Carlo is transported by the beauty of the language, a return of compliments between God and man. At the same time he is moved by the ordinariness of human grieving and the way it is set against the sublimity of the service. The ceremony for the dead, he decides, is an art form deftly designed to enable the fact of death to be registered by the living. What flourishes also withers, but by a supreme act of faith we overcome death. The chalice is elevated, and we who might otherwise be defeated by mortality have the promise of the resurrection.

The priests, each carrying a lighted candle, now lead the coffin from the church and the procession falls in behind. Carlo looks out over a sea of faces with rippling eyes all turned towards him. Here and there he picks out familiar features, lineaments from long ago, reminders of another time gilded by his beloved mother.

Memories flow unbidden into his head of languorous days when the grapes were sweetening on the vine and the atmosphere was thick with the dry chatter of cicadas. He can hear his mother calling to him now from across the fields of orange blossom and banks of time. Was it really so? Or have the harsh contours of childhood simply been softened by sentiment and the sorrow he now feels? Carlo lacks the strength to decide.

Amidst the rows of old women in black shawls, some with handkerchiefs tied at the nape of their necks, he is surprised by a spectre of loveliness, separated by age and aspect from those around her. Her dark head is bowed, dimming her features. For one fleeting second he thinks it might be a mirage of his mother come like a ministering angel to take away his pain. In the next instant he knows it is the woman who lit the candle in church.

The cold space under his ribs is gently warmed as the procession passes from the solemn shade of the church to the glare of the afternoon sun on the piazza. At the cemetery people kneel briefly at the coffin, some leaving candles, others reciting the rosary, before dispersing to pay respects to their own dead. The mood is lighter, almost festive, and slender smiles wipe away tears. Only the family lingers, an amorphous assembly gathered round the mortal remains. '*Requiescat in pace* . . . May she rest in peace.' With these words the life of Carlo's mother is surrendered to the great mystery of death, and for a moment, or so it seems to her eldest son, all the world stands still. *He has met with his mother for the last time.*

Five

In the night following the day of the funeral Carlo cannot sleep. Away from the protection of the church and the comfort of the Requiem Mass he is like a boat drifting rudderless in an ocean of despair. The Aristotelian catharsis has eluded him. After the emotion of the ceremony and the sheer pathos of the final farewell, he had hoped perhaps to be purged of his grief and released into some quiet calm place where he could piece together the shards of his broken spirit.

Instead he feels there is nothing he can do with his suffering except to suffer it. And where is God amidst all this misery? Presiding over the business of death, Carlo imagines, and lulling us into a dutiful acceptance of it. Carlo feels angry and betrayed, tired of playing the religious game which involves so much pain. Little wonder that Dostoevsky has Ivan Karamazov return his ticket to God because the miserable sinner has no respect for the rules of religion. Carlo is suddenly appalled by the outrage which God has committed against man, and the absolute impotence of his own mortal coil. How to make sense of it all?

He feels a desperate need for exegesis, a desire to deal systematically with what has happened. He remembers reading that in Roman times there were professional exegetes — people employed as official interpreters of omens, charms, dreams, sacred law and oracular pronouncements. If only he were better equipped to read the signs; if only he possessed the wisdom of the oracle. Instead he feels more like some poor latter-day iconoclast, questioning cherished beliefs on his own pot-holed path to enlightenment.

He lies in bed now, but like a mortally wounded man who reports a feeling of partial separation from his suffering body, Carlo seems to be somewhere else, looking down on himself, trying to penetrate the unfathomable. He wants to understand his grief and experience it not as pain, but as knowledge. Knowledge is strength, and he believes that if only he can get to the heart of his sorrow, understand its basis, the secret will be revealed; and thus empowered he will be healed and made whole again.

But instead of knowledge he feels in the grip of invincible ignorance. To be in ignorance, he thinks, might be a perfectly tolerable state provided one perceived it as something else – such as awareness (he can think of many people who live in this way and lead quite untroubled lives); but to be aware of one's own benightedness – that is surely a living torment. At the same time Carlo is filled with self-loathing at his introspection, his concentration on self, his preoccupation with the implications of his mother's death for his own life. He seems to be moving within a landscape whose only point of reference is his own well-being.

Everything that has happened since the funeral has served to emphasize and increase his feeling of separation, of otherness, of alienation. He does not belong here among these people who are now behaving so *normally*. They engage in daily chores like cooking and cleaning and loading the washing-machine. They chat with each other, laugh with each other, just as if everything is perfectly all right and no one has died.

To make matters worse they make anodyne comments like 'She is at peace now', or 'She has gone to a better place', as if they were meaningful statements. These remarks, born of uncertainty but uttered with total conviction, are designed to comfort, to put up smokescreens, but they fill Carlo with a kind of impotent rage. His urbaneness requires him to smile and nod in tacit agreement, but he blazes inside.

When his dear kind sister-in-law says, 'She is with God now', he wants to scream a barrage of questions: 'Oh yes, and where exactly is *that*? And in what sense do you mean *is*? Not surely in the sense that I *am*, or you *are*. Not in the bodily sense, because in case you've forgotten, we buried her remains earlier today in the cemetery wall. And what could *now* possibly mean, except a point on our own human time scale? Surely being dead, if it means anything at all, means being beyond time as we know it, being outside of time, beyond paltry mortal distinctions between past and present and future.' None of this does he say of course; and he feels further defeated by his own self-imposed dumbness.

In truth he envies them their certainty, their uncritical acceptance of God and death and the Resurrection. Of course he imbibed with his mother's milk the same beliefs as they did; as a child he breathed in that same ineffable attitude to the world which cannot be acquired or learned later in life. What has happened since then? Somehow the old words and ways have deserted him; or perhaps it is he who has forsaken them.

Whom God would destroy He first makes mad. Is that what is happening to him? If only his wife were here, his beloved Flora. And yet he had not wanted her to come, almost as if he knew it was a journey he had to make alone. He must get back to her quickly, to feel the tenderness of her touch, the constancy of her affection, the dependability which comes of a long and happy marriage. Like a mother with a fretful child, she will soothe and comfort and make him better. She will make his recovery possible.

★ ★ ★

Flora, hello! It's me. I'm sorry to ring so late.

Like a fountain of goodness, she spouts gentle words of sympathy and concern, thinking not of herself, only of him and his difficulties. She wonders if it has been *very* hard for him, and of course she has been thinking of him, *poor dear*, and wondering how it all went. The English language suddenly seems to him so poised, so temperate, so perfunctory even.

Yes, I'm fine, thanks.

(Why is it easier to lie?) She feels for him so much. It must have been *simply awful* for him. It is a very difficult time. He must be very kind to himself. She *does* hope everything went well. (The power of love is awesome, even when it is imperfect, conditional. Perhaps only a mother's love is unconditional.)

Well, you know what funerals are like. Not much fun at the best of times.

He's doing it too, joining in the linguistic game

of understatement. She responds lovingly, solicitously. And also practically, remembering to give progress reports on the conservatory and the garden and the children's preparation for exams. She sounds absolutely in command of herself and her situation. (He has to remind himself that these are the qualities which first attracted her to him. It all seems such a long time ago.) She is loving and gracious, and does not forget to tell him how much she is missing him, how much she is looking forward to his coming back.

Darling, I'm afraid I'm going to have to stay on for a few days. These things are done rather differently in Italy. It will look bad if I take off immediately.

Of course she understands completely (and not at all), and tells him not to worry. His colleagues at work are bound to be sympathetic, even though things never run as smoothly when he's away. But it can't be helped, and they'll just have to manage without him for a few more days. And everything is fine at home. She has repainted the bathroom, she is busy in the garden, and her diet is going well – she has lost three whole pounds. She feels like a new woman.

I love you, Flora.

Men and women are not strong enough to live their lives alone. Many people try to persuade themselves differently, but their existence is harrowed by loneliness and lovelessness.

★ ★ ★

There is a gulf which divides all human beings from each other, even those with whom we are most intimate. Carlo feels that gulf now as never before. He believes that privacy is essential to all but the shallowest of marriages, and in hiding his distress from his wife he feels he has honoured that belief in some measure. What he fears is the indignity of exposure, the unmasking of his soul, even to the woman he loves.

Since the phone call he feels a new dimension of despair. Even the warmest kind of communication can be conducted in a mist of apprehension.

Signs are given and interpreted wrongly; or they are not given, and are therefore presumed not to exist. The possibility for obfuscation is almost limitless. Why did he tell her he had to stay on? He does not know any more — it was just what he said. He is beginning to feel that there is more to his state of mind than the loss of his mother. Once again he is afraid of what is happening to him.

When his father died he felt very little; but in later years he came to believe that some element of truth had departed the world with him. Now with his mother gone, he feels that some of life's beauty has been eclipsed. Truth and beauty — what else remains? Love, of course; the love of his wife, the love of his children. Carlo knows at a very deep level of his being that in loving and in being loved he is twice blessed. It is true that marriage has modified his passion, rather than nourished it, but this is exactly as he would wish it, because passion leads to chaos and uncontrollable feelings. Unfortunately the outward equanimity he has worked so hard to achieve belies the clamour within. His thoughts are no longer hiding-places for his feelings. He has tried to live by reason, but reason now seems like a cruel refinement on the coarseness of the human condition.

It seems inconceivable that she is dead, that she should be gone not just yesterday and today, but for the next day and every day after that, and all possible days. And to think that death has not yet revealed its full force, its capacity to wreak havoc on those left behind. It is still in its infancy, still only a day or two old, and its short shadow is sure to lengthen and eclipse the pall-bearer. Everything feels over, done with, finished, and there is nothing he can do about it. *He must bear his cross.*

Six

The white ant, in spite of its name, is rarely white. It assumes rather the colour of the earth in which it lives. Neither is it, properly speaking, an ant at all, but a termite. It is the precursor of man on the planet earth by some one hundred million years, a fact which has been established by the discovery of numerous specimens in fossil amber. Next to man its civilisation is the most complex of any species. Indeed some would argue that it is superior to that of man.

The termitary is a construction of amazing ingenuity. It is a series of colossal multi-storeyed catacombs, linked by an intricate network of corridors and tunnels. On the surface it sometimes resembles a huge rambling ancient castle with buttresses and battlements, radiating like the branches of trees, powerful enough to deter the most hostile invader. The termitary is built from the inside out, although the way in which this is done is not yet perfectly understood. No one has ever been able to observe one being built, but it is a largely subterranean structure, and what appears on the surface, although vast, is of secondary importance.

The building material starts off as a kind of slime which is passed through the intestine of the white ant emerging as a white powder with properties superior to those of cement. It is marvellously fertile (trees sometimes sprout on top of the colony); it will not disintegrate when animals stampede over it, nor when cars collide with it (though damage to the vehicle may be considerable); and it is unaffected by heavy tropical rainstorms which are a feature of the areas in which it is found.

The disproportion between the size of the termitary and the termites who build it almost beggars belief. Translated to our own human scale the average termitary would correspond to a building over six hundred metres high, something which of course has never been attempted by man.

In Queensland, for reasons which are not yet fully understood, the dwellings always face exactly north and south, the broad part to the south, the narrower to the north. White ants live mostly in equatorial regions (although there are some poor relations to be found in Sicily), but by some perverse stroke of fate they die if they are exposed to the sun. As a rule they have no wings, but those who do are cruelly endowed, since they are allowed just one brief flight to certain death.

They are also absolutely dependent on moisture, yet they manage to live in countries where rainfall is limited to a few months of the year. This led Dr David Livingstone to remark to Stanley, when they met on the banks of Lake Tanganyika in 1871, that perhaps by some method as yet unknown to man they managed to combine the oxygen of the atmosphere with the hydrogen of their vegetable food, thereby replacing in the degree of its evaporation their requirements for water. This hypothesis has not yet been improved upon.

In the most adverse circumstances the white ant has adapted itself to its egregious situation. It is the most disinherited of creatures. It has no eyes, no wings, no weapons (such as a sting), and because of a system of voluntary castration, no sex. Yet it has overcome the impoverishment of its condition and emerged from its wretchedness to become the most tenacious, the most formidable inhabitant of our planet. Compared to the white ant, man may be considered limited, imperfect, ignorant.

* * *

'I'm sorry, I must be boring you. I tend to get completely carried away when I talk about this.'

Carlo is not at all bored. He is sitting with Petra at a café table outside in the piazza, but his fascination with this woman whom he has known for less than twenty minutes is so inordinate that he is almost oblivious of his surroundings.

He knows very little about her except that she lives in Naples where she works in the department of anthropology at the university. She is spending a few weeks here with her parents (who, he discovers, were acquainted with his mother) while recovering from a bout of illness induced by overworking. She had suddenly appeared beside him, introduced herself, and offered her condolences; he had extended his hand and, with a formal gesture, motioned to the chair opposite him. In response to his awkward enquiry about her job (the standard English social prelim: '*And what do you do?*'), she had smiled, tossed back her hair with her slender fingers, and told him her area of research — the inner life of the celibate priest —

and how her academic journey had started with a study of another great celibate — the white ant.

He is completely transported by her story, not just by the information she conveys, but by the way in which she tells it. What might easily have been a dry academic discourse is told with a passion and zeal which would shame the keenest executives in his own profession. He mutters something about it being a fascinating subject, which comes out as token politeness, although he means every word. He asks her to tell him more. She possesses none of his diffidence, and with a smile and another toss of her head she begins to describe the plight of the white ant.

'This creature seems in many ways to be so highly developed, yet it leads the most shackled of existences, never seeing the light of day, condemned to everlasting darkness. In relation to the bee — although the hive is no stranger to tragedy — its life is incomparably more wretched. At least with the bee we imagine there to be earthly joys, such as light and space and sunshine, the fragrance of flowers and its wonderful honeyed palace; and of course bees have wings to help them enjoy these delights. But with the termite there is unrelieved blackness, unequalled tyranny and submission, limitless sacrifice.'

Her voice modulates to accommodate the pity of her subject and her eyes seem to moisten in sympathy. Carlo thinks he has never heard such eloquence, such felicity of expression married to an area of investigation he has never before considered. It is entirely beyond his own experience of the world, but she has breathed such life into it as to make him completely entranced and absorbed.

– Do we have anything in common with the white ant?

'There are certainly comparisons to be made, and this is where it becomes really interesting. We have to consider what the point of the termitary is. Have the white ants been living for millions of years simply for the sake of surviving and perpetuating the miseries of their existence? But this question is perhaps too anthropocentric. I mean, who are we to say that their existence is miserable and without point? In some ways the white ants can be said to know more than we do. They are tirelessly inventive, they are biologists and chemists, and they operate a form of communism beyond our wildest imagination.'

Carlo is rapt. The story Petra relates is utterly marvellous. There is no need — as in Carlo's advertising business — to dress it up; the reality is a marvel in itself. He believes he is on the brink of hearing something of great significance, something which perhaps has implications even for his own life. He is anxious to understand everything this fascinating woman is telling him.

— I'm not sure I know what you mean.

'Well, everything is sacrificed for the common good: their sex, their wings, their eyes. They renounce any individuality or personal gain for the sake of their fellow creatures. The workers in the colony adopt all the pastoral roles, and much more besides — they are builders, gardeners, gatherers, architects, doctors, undertakers. They eat and digest for everybody. The warriors, male and female, resist to the death any breach in the termitary. There is no waste: everything comes from their own bodies; even their excrement is used and re-used indefinitely. Their submission to laws is quite without equal in human society, and their discipline far stricter than in the most enclosed of monastic orders. It is tempting to ascribe their intricate organization and high level of sophistication to the force of nature. But this is to evade the real questions. As an explanation it is too simple.'

Petra's dark hair, parted in the middle, falls down nearly to her bare shoulders. Her delicate neck is encircled by a band of coral from which hangs a small silver cross. Her eyes are bright and animated.

– Why is it too simple?

'We tend to think that everything which is deep and great and complex must have a human provenance. Man considers himself to be the standard against which all living creatures have to be measured. But intellect is not limited to human beings; there are almost certainly other kinds of intellect – why should our own be accorded a higher status? The white ants practise discipline and self-sacrifice – generally perceived to be virtues in human terms – but because they are thought to be obeying some natural law, because they are blind and instinctive we tend not to consider them valiant or noble. By what right, by what knowledge do we do this?'

Carlo feels quite humbled by the power of Petra's exposition. He is captivated by the wonder of it all. Not since he sat at the feet of Sister Ignatia, listening to her describe how bees visit the sweetest-smelling flowers in order to produce the wax from which the holy candles are made, has he felt such rapture.

— Our own attempts at communism have usually been doomed . . .

'The white ants have succeeded where often we have failed. They have adapted their own miserable attributes and created marvellous underground citadels whose constitution and civilisation are not at all arbitrary. There is no rest, they never sleep, and illness is not tolerated. Their sacrifice is such that by our lights they would be regarded as heroes and heroines. Like those called to serve God they practise the strictest of vows: poverty, obedience and chastity, but even the most self-punishing ascetic has never opted for blindness and darkness.'

She is like a garden in full bloom, her words full of different shapes and colours. Her mobile face dances in concert with her shining eyes. She is speaking mostly in English (she has spent two years researching in Australia and lectures in English all over the world), but every so often she effervesces into a stream of Italian. The combination is captivating.

— Are there lessons we can learn from the white ant?

'The truth is we have not yet fathomed the mysteries of the termitary. Of course we can speculate on the evidence of what we see, but it is difficult not to judge the evidence purely in relation to our own lives. We can attribute the phenomenon of the termitary to some intelligence or directing force; or to the genius of nature, to Providence, to evolution, or to blind chance; or we can attribute it to God. In the most highly regarded systems of human morality, man struggles and suffers in order to be redeemed and purified and exalted. To be sure the white ant is no stranger to struggle and suffering, but we have to ask ourselves if the striving has any point other than continuance of the species.'

Her eyes are ablaze now, and her hands too have come alive. He is intoxicated with her devotion to her subject. This is a woman with a mission, a vocation no less than the Sisters of Santa Scholastica. But she also possesses qualities which they lacked; a sophistication, an awareness, a sensuality, all of which connect her to the secular world.

– And what do you yourself think?

'As an academic I have to deal in verifiable facts and undisputed evidence. This is the clear duty of the researcher. But facts are also subject to interpretation – even historical events are interpreted differently. And so as an interested observer whose emotions are involved, I am inclined to believe that the life of the white ant, more than any other creature, is an epitome for our own. Its destiny prefigures ours, its struggle has been going on for millions of years before we even came into existence. But there is not a shred of evidence to suggest that its fortunes have improved, that its endless labours have been rewarded. And the same, I would suggest, applies to man, who is no nearer to God than when he started out.'

— So where does that leave us?

'We have not even begun to understand why we are alive, why we are on this earth, why we have to endure so much before being released by death. We postulate, but we cannot prove. This intellect of ours has enabled us only to comprehend that ultimately everything is incomprehensible. Don't worry — that is not the cynical conclusion that it might appear to be. Both the white ant and man seem to be governed by a mysterious power which guides them and influences their lives. If we accept the enigma of that, then it is a liberation, and we are free to respond to the enigma in whatever way may *seem* to improve our condition, enhance our lives, nourish our spirits. It may be an illusion, we may not ever find the answers, but we must keep seeking; otherwise man will be driven to despair. This is one reason why we must not mock our religion. Those who believe they are called to God are addressing the questions for all of us.'

Petra has touched him at a very deep level. Her eyes are still bright and she continues to smile despite the seriousness of her subject. She has made things seem not only tolerable, but exciting and challenging. Poignant of course, but not beyond hope. At this moment he has no thought for his own individual struggle, his own pain; both now seem entirely bearable. *A hand has wiped the cares from his face.*

Seven

The choices people make determine to some extent who they are. If they recognize that they have the freedom to choose, then they have the possibility to act in good or bad faith. Those who accept the notion of free will usually distinguish further between what they ought to do and what they are inclined to do. In this respect moral laws provide some degree of constraint on human behaviour.

For Carlo and Petra, however, as they set off for their picnic in the hills, this distinction is quite blurred. If there be such a concept as the right thing to do, objectively speaking, they both feel themselves to be engaged in it; moreover, although their perspectives may differ, they feel not so much that they are exercising a choice as obeying a commandment.

In southern Italy time still seems to be the servant of man, not the master, and although the town bustles with the usual Saturday market, it retains a relaxed and easygoing cheerfulness. The main piazza, garnished with clusters of bougainvillaea and powder-puffs of spiraea, is crowded with push-carts and tables which groan with local produce. There are stalls of saffron and wine, olives and cheese, and buyers and sellers alike seem to bubble with the eagerness of a new day. There are blithe calls of '*Buon giorno!*' and '*Ciao!*'. Children play at the fountain, and even the old men at café tables hoist their waistbands and seem reinvigorated. Everything has a gilded edge.

Carlo and Petra leave the square which gives on to narrow alleys with snakes and ladders boards of balustered stairways. Lines of bunting bearing motley washing are strung between balconies, and doorways the colour of verdigris are flanked by trailing plants in heavy earthenware pots. The road leading out of town winds flat through the fields before rising steeply into the hillside. Carlo looks back at the medieval roofs, a quilt of variegated browns, and sees his birthplace bathed in a strange alchemy of nostalgia and intensification.

Away from the town the noises are different: the tuneless tinkle of a distant cowbell, the click clack of a woodcutter's axe, the shrill warning of a jay. The road is deserted apart from an old woman who limps past carrying a basket of hens. On one side is a regiment of carefully tended saplings standing to attention, on the other a carnival of wild flowers. The road soon gives way to a dusty track rutted by cartwheels. The sun is exuberant and wraps the hillside in a golden cloak. Higher up there are rows of vines supported by white sticks, like old blind men wilting in the sun.

Twenty-four hours have passed since their animated conversation in the piazza. For Carlo it has brought about an enlargement of the world; for Petra a confirmation of her initial desire. As they amble along the scorched track their exchanges seem to be rather formal, picking up where they left off on the larger questions arising from Petra's research; as if by some tacit agreement they will thereby avoid anything too intimate. But the nature of irony is such that the most fastidious series of questions and answers reveals more about their inner feelings than any calculated attempt at familiarity might do. Their dialogue resembles two rivers rising close to one another, sometimes following roughly parallel courses for a stretch, sometimes diverging in different directions only to meet again round another bend.

It is true that their personal lives have barely been touched upon, although they have both made known their marriages. Petra has referred fleetingly to hers in the soft tones of resignation, signalling lost hope and private sadness; Carlo has declared his as a simple fact. He feels no sense of disloyalty; rather he imagines himself to be standing on the brink of some exciting new discovery, like a man sailing in uncharted waters. He experiences none of the fear of the explorer, only the exhilaration; it is as if he has reached a new understanding of the world, or at least a new interpretation which allows him to act truly and freely for the first time. Like Blake he feels he is uncovering the secrets of a land unknown.

As the sun climbs in the sky Petra and Carlo head towards the relative cool of the olive grove which beckons like a green and silver oasis. Carlo stops to look down at the town which seems quite distant now and shimmers in the heat like a busy weaver's loom. Not far off he can see a stooped shepherd isolated from his flock and fellow man. Carlo turns to follow Petra. She is wearing a sleeveless shirt of pale blue silk and a white skirt which ripples as she walks. Her little spiral hat sits askew on her head like a careless mollusc on a rock. He experiences a kind of longing, not painful or disabling, but somehow noble and pure.

They move deep into the grove and sit beneath a large tree whose branches entwine like the sinuous limbs of lovers. In the manner of a ritual preparation for a sacred act, they spread a thin cotton sheet over the carpet of leaves, and in a moment of intense emotion they look into each other's eyes with trust and beneficence. It is the genesis of love.

★ ★ ★

The merging of two bodies is the most beautiful form of elision. At first they lie side by side, hands gently touching, hearts beating to the frenzied crossfire of cicadas. He is half-mad with delight and desire. He raises himself on his elbow, and turns towards her. She lies bathed in that penumbra of perfection which is given only to the most perfect works of art.

Although he has supposed it all morning, he now sees quite clearly that she is wearing nothing beneath her shirt. Deftly, but with that discreet diffidence which characterizes English reserve, he undoes her buttons to reveal her pale soft breasts. He touches her nipples which instantly burgeon like hyacinth buds. Their lips meet and they kiss the novice kisses of new beginnings, new possibilities, new convictions.

Strong and gentle as the waves, he swells and moves towards her like the sea to the shore. He dips and dives, eagerly but hesitantly, still fearing rebuff, until that moment of absolute clarification, when her ardour too is confirmed beyond doubt. Her lissom limbs quiver and enfold him in the sticky deliciousness of her sex. Carlo and Petra are on the threshold of another state of being which does not depend on illusion or reasoning or artifice; but is its own joy. It is known only to those who experience it, and cannot be discovered vicariously.

He probes at her soft folds, innocent and beautiful beyond imagination. Everything is liquid and loosened. Droplets of moisture sit on her copper fleece like morning dew on a resplendent frond. In the moment before they connect and surrender he sees his soul's desire reflected in her dark bright eyes. In a spasm of ecstasy he slips and slides and sinks into the silken gulf. Fire within fire. The beat inside her rises and quickens, impelling both of them to the edge of the world. A honeyed fusion of bodies and spirits, a melody of sweet abandonment, and the whole hillside begins to sing in chorus as he sobs his ejaculation. *And falls.*

Eight

However much we may demur, we are hitched to a world in which actions beget consequences. At some level we are all called upon to answer for what we have done, though of course the scale and extent may vary considerably. However, as Carlo and Petra come down from their nest on the hillside, this empirical truth is furthest from their minds. Their lovemaking has conferred upon them a special dispensation from the world of actions and consequences. They are in that post-coital state of grace, which frees them completely from the otherwise unyielding chain of cause and effect.

Their bodies, saturated with heat and prolonged lovemaking, move differently now. They are no longer constrained by purpose or deployed in the merely practical, like walking to get from A to B, or bending to pick up a stone; they move for the sheer pleasure of moving, and with a new grace. Both lovers have a fresh consciousness of shape and form, their own and each other's, which now seem elegant and exalted.

Petra appears to Carlo to possess all the qualities of a consummate work of art, and his eyes now feast on her as they would on a canonical masterpiece. He has long believed that all great artists have glimpsed heaven, if heaven is defined as that blessed place beyond the ordinary understanding of most men and women. And those who are privileged to see the artists' great works – even if they do not themselves glimpse heaven – are accorded their own moment of epiphany.

Carlo's moment of epiphany seems to be a place of infinite time, space and possibility. He and Petra have spent nearly the whole day on the hillside, though the normal time-scale has not applied. In their strange state of heightened happiness, when the hours are filled with beauty and ecstasy, each hour seems like an entire day.

Carlo feels he understands everything about the

world now, all that is good, all that is bad; and that he apprehends it in a new way. Once again his life has been turned upside down. As with his mother's death, everything is altered; but instead of being distorted by the agony of bereavment, all is transfigured by the power of love. The tension between the fixed immutable structure of his mind and the soft sensitive contours of his heart is unexpectedly resolved.

'Beauty is truth, truth beauty,' — that is all / Ye know on earth, and all ye need to know. He occupies that incandescent realm unveiled to lovers throughout centuries, where every blade of grass, every leaf, every gesture and movement is endowed with a Keatsian beauty. He looks in wonder at his surroundings, with the ingenuousness of a child.

There are times when the outer physical world seems perfectly to reflect the inner; as Carlo surveys the sweep of the landscape the magnificence of what he sees seems to match supremely the interior of his spirit. It is revelatory, mystical. He feels completed, made whole, as if some missing part has been returned.

Such is the poetry in his soul, he imagines this ordinary little Italian hill could be Mount Parnassus itself. And the dusty track which they now walk along, arm in arm, could be a band of liquid gold. Of course he is enough of a realist to know that these are fanciful thoughts; but he also knows at some profound level that they are the fruits of a rare passion, and as such they constitute another reality, not revealed to everyone, but admissible nonetheless.

The surprising thing for Carlo is that he feels no guilt. Neither has he any sense of being the architect of his own downfall, because he has no perception of dishonour or shame; nor, therefore, does he experience remorse. (Still less does he feel a victim of circumstances, which he would not wish to alter in any detail.) Indeed he feels entirely innocent, utterly pure in heart, returned – by some mysterious anomaly – to a state of virginity. He smiles at the central absurdity of this thought, but is quite unable to abandon it.

Far from feeling he has lost his bearings, he believes that his bearings have shifted and clarified. He is raised above the banality of everyday living to something extraordinary and limitless. Can it be that through an act of infidelity (because he knows in some darkling recess of his mind that is what it is) he has come closer to God?

It is too early to wonder what lies ahead. But he does not see his lovemaking with Petra as an isolated, inconsequential event. He feels that such a love happens only very rarely; and when it does it is more precious than anything else. He has no inkling that it will end in pain and deception. He does not yet know that he has entered a domain of passionate chaos of proportions hitherto unknown to him; or that it is a domain which betokens the end of inocence and hope. For the moment everything is gilded in the beautiful light he casts upon it. He feels purified, cleansed, possessed of a clarity of purpose. *Weep not for him.*

Nine

Everything is both clouded and clarified by lovemaking. Petra has been under such strain recently — overtired, overworked — and now the tension has all but disappeared, the *tightness* in her body completely gone. She marvels at the way in which such intense physical activity can impose calm and heal the spirit. Petra's experience of life, however, together with her academic interests, have taught her that nothing in the area of sex is at all straightforward.

Her religion is extremely important to her, but she has spent much of her adult life trying to come to terms with Catholic teaching on the sinfulness of the flesh. Although she loves her Church she deplores the tortuous attitudes to sex which have dominated its teaching since earliest times.

The early Church Fathers have a lot to answer for. St Jerome – not a favourite of Petra's – set the pattern by lamenting the immodesty and lasciviousness of women. He wrote fiery invectives on the subject and was regarded as being very wise and learned. Then St Augustine, whose thinking prevailed for centuries, convinced everyone that the root of all evil was concupiscence. And since women inspired concupiscence, they became *ipso facto* irredeemably associated with evil.

One of the consequences for the faithful is that at many points throughout history, salvation has depended on chastity, and damnation has been inextricably linked with female licentiousness. All manner of stringent methods – obedience, submission, virginity, domesticity – have been advocated to limit and prevent sexual activity. Although in the late twentieth century many of the strictures have relaxed, Petra believes that it is partly residual guilt which makes modern relationships so problematic.

It is not that she feels especially persecuted as a woman. She knows perfectly well that men have also been subject to the moral guardianship of the church. The fundamental view throughout the ages that sexual relations are somehow 'unclean' has affected men no less than women. In the course of her studies of celibacy, for example, Petra has waded through many volumes of moral theology devoted to the problem of what are delicately called 'nocturnal emissions'. These massive tomes might make comic reading had the consequences for the clergy not been so serious.

The theology is based on the so-called pollution theory, whereby any priest who experienced such an emission in his sleep would not be in a state of purity to celebrate the Eucharist the following day. (It was later decreed that an emission would not be morally polluting provided the priest did not wake up and enjoy it.) This issue seems to have caused much the same amount of highly charged – and, Petra thinks, largely hysterical – debate as the more recent furore in England over women priests.

Although she is well aware of the multiplicity of theological arguments against the ordination of women priests, she cannot help thinking that the main objection rests on another taboo: menstruation. This is difficult to prove of course, but it is certainly the case that long after a taboo has officially been discarded, its influence continues to be felt. And Petra knows from private discussions with many of the Catholic clergy that the thought of receiving the sacrament from a menstruating woman would be more than their sensibilities could bear. Of course it suits the purpose of those opposed to women priests to appeal to scripture and the undeniable fact that God was made incarnate only as a man. But actually it is the idea of a priest with a period which is unthinkable.

Petra thinks it a great pity that the Church has always had such a problem with vital fluids like semen and menstrual blood. Her own theory is that it is man, not God, who has difficulty with natural emissions. Just as it is man, not God, who has such awful trouble with women's sexuality (and occasionally his own). This is not simply a religious problem; it has entered our culture and is reflected in our literature. It is no accident that our literary classics portray largely domestic heroines; or that those, like Anna Karenina or Madame Bovary, who do not conform to the accepted paradigm of womanhood, generally pay the penalty.

Petra has given a great deal of thought to these

matters. Unlike some of her feminist colleagues at the university, she has never been particularly inclined to put all the blame for women's problems onto men. For one thing she believes that men have also been victims of the Church's preoccupation with sexual issues. Of course ever since Eve's misbehaviour, women have been accused of leading men astray. But men — and she includes her husband here — have nevertheless had to cope with the general climate; and the climate has never been conducive to guilt-free copulation. Petra thinks it is far better for men and women to work together to improve matters, than for women to write petulant feminist tracts about personal growth without the need for male companions.

In the light of all these considerations Petra has developed a largely pragmatic approach to sex. She long ago decided that sex, like suffering, was part of the human condition. But unlike suffering, it was there to be enjoyed. This need not offend those who believe that it is primarily intended for the purposes of procreation. But when not procreating, why not enjoy? As a theory it is deliciously simple, and she likes to think that it also has the imprimatur of God who, when all is said and done, *designed* us as sexual creatures.

In her more mature years, therefore, Petra has attempted to work out a code of practice based primarily on considerations for her own health and well-being, rather than the religious culture in which she lives. Far better to acknowledge her sexuality and deal with it sensibly, than to lock it away like a mad relative in the attic and allow it to wreak havoc in secret.

Her marriage confers a number of benefits, but sexual satisfaction is not one of them. The fact that she and her husband have no children has become an increasing difficulty, exacerbated by a total lack of open discussion on the subject. Her husband naturally assumes that she is the infertile partner. For the sake of his feelings she does not demur; but she knows from medical tests that it has no basis in fact.

Childlessness, particularly in a country like Italy, is always perceived as a negative state – a disappointment, a loss, a non-fulfilment of purpose. In the less enlightened south it can even be considered culpable. Petra has managed to come to terms with all of this, but her husband has found it deeply emasculating. It has certainly not improved their sexual relations.

Petra's career and professional interests have compensated to a large extent for the limitations of her marriage. As a good-looking professional woman in her late thirties she is quite often the subject of men's attentions, but she makes it a rule not to become intimately involved with her colleagues. This does not stop *her* feeling attracted to *them* of course. Indeed she regularly experiences the most ungovernable feelings of lust. On these occasions, even if she is at work, she simply closes her office door, reclines in the soft armchair, and fantasises about the man in question till she reaches a climax. In fact some of her most intense orgasms have been self-induced, and she considers the health benefits of regular relief to be beyond dispute.

Aside from solitary sex and her marital relations (which rarely bring her to climax) Petra has occasional and wonderful liaisons, mostly at academic conferences, which generally offer very favourable conditions for coupling. These encounters are nearly always short-lived, and therefore fairly innocuous. Unlike St Augustine she does not believe that confession is good for the soul. Nor is it good for one's spouse. Petra knows her husband would be quite unable to accept any suggestion of infidelity on her part. As with most men his pride and self-esteem would not be able to withstand such an assault. (He, to Petra's certain knowledge, has slept with many women, but this is a complex area, and different standards apply.) And so it is principally to spare his feelings that Petra chooses not to tell, rather than from any basic impulse to deceive. She also loves him.

With Carlo, however, some of her own carefully worked out ground rules seem to be under threat. For one thing she feels uncommonly *drawn* to him, partly because he intrigues her so much. For a high-powered advertising executive he has an exceptional degree of sensitivity. He is also complex and serious and strangely vulnerable, qualities Petra has always found extremely seductive. When he reaches his climax he makes a curious sobbing sound which is erotic beyond description, and reminds her of his weeping in the church. Can it have been only a few days ago? Her sense of time is completely blurred by passion. Secondly — or perhaps she means firstly — he is an exceptionally competent and considerate lover. His vigour and gentleness are quite without equal in her experience. Apart from the sheer physical pleasure he gives her, he has taken possession of that still centre of her being, which she cannot see but whose existence is not in doubt.

She already knows it will be difficult to give him up.

* * *

— *I love you, Petra.*

— *Don't you think it's too soon for love?*

— *There are so many different kinds of love, of course. And what I feel for you is only a few days old. But I still want to call it love.*

— *You will be gone in a day or two. So shall I. It will be as if nothing ever happened.*

— *Don't say that. Please don't say that.*

— *We mustn't get too involved.*

— *We* are *involved.*

— *But we shouldn't lose sight of the facts. We're both married . . . we live in different countries . . . there can be no future.*

— *I don't want to give you up . . . I can't give you up.*

— *Try not to think of it as giving up. Think of it as letting go . . .*

* * *

Carlo feels driven, possessed. He is in the grip of some mysterious energy which has surged out of nowhere and taken charge of his mind and body. He has ceased to be in control, he answers to a new set of rules, a different morality applies to the world. He is convinced that what he is experiencing is unique. Petra has cast a magical spell over him, and he minds not at all. Each time he makes love he enters a timeless realm, and his stay there, however brief, leaves him altered. It would be difficult to say precisely how he is changed; but what he has discovered with Petra is a different dimension of himself and a wondrous enlargement of the world. Simple, profound, and beautiful beyond words. *He has definitively fallen.*

Ten

However love is defined, it invariably includes the notion that it is something *substantial*, that it has the power to change lives. Somehow it abrogates the notion of self-determination and replaces it with kind of fatalism. Carlo thinks there is no point in trying to resist it; he must simply bend to its power.

What he feels for Petra is a fledgling love, and as such it contains great promise. It is his hope for the future. Each time they make love the hope is affirmed and reaffirmed. She is also his link with the past, the innocence of his childhood, the essence of his homeland. She is his former life, the solace of religion, his *alter ego*. She is passionate and loving and — here he hesitates a little — wonderfully *maternal*. There is a softness in her love which is motherly and nourishing, and in her presence the pain of bereavement is immaterial. She furnishes his mind, she governs his dreams, she fills his imagination.

His body is quite exhausted from the exertions of lovemaking, but when he and Petra are together the magnetic force between them seems inexorable, ordained. In the brief intervals when they are apart — when she calls at her parents' house, for example — he counts the minutes till he will see her again. He even writes love letters or poems to make the separation more bearable. As soon as they are together again he gives her what he has written. She smiles as she reads, and her smile melts his heart.

The future, insofar as he imagines it at all, is a sun-filled place, undefiled by difficulties or problems. He sees it still as a general amorphous thing, not delineated with any precision. It will contain Petra of course, and Flora and the children. These are the essential ingredients. Everything beyond is indeterminate.

At odd moments, in between lovemaking, he wonders how he will tell Flora.

★ ★ ★

— *Flora, it's me.*

— *Darling, how lovely to hear you. I've been thinking of you such a lot.*

— *And I'm thinking of you.*

— *How are things going? You sound a bit down.*

— *No, I'm not at all. It's just that things are taken rather longer than I thought.*

— *Well, I suppose that's what happens. As the eldest son, I expect there's more for you to do. Try not to let it get you down. You'll be home soon.*

— *Flora, you know I love you.*

— *Yes, darling, of course I do. I expect you're missing all of us. The boys send their love, by the way.*

— *But Flora, I want you to know, I do love you. Never forget that.*

— *Darling, are you sure you're all right?*

— *Of course. I'm absolutely fine. I just wanted you to know.*

* * *

At some point he will have to *explain* his behaviour to Flora. He will have to describe a sequence of actions which will add up to something she can understand. As yet he has no idea of how this will be possible.

Supposing he tells the simple truth. But what exactly does telling the truth entail? Does it mean describing exactly what happened in factual terms? What precisely has the truth to do with facts? In this case very little, he thinks. He rehearses it now in his mind, and immediately everything becomes distorted in the process of articulation.

I saw Petra for the first time in church, then she turned up at Mother's funeral. The next day we talked over coffee in the piazza. And the day after that we went walking in the hills where we made love all afternoon. These are the facts, but they convey nothing of the truth.

He contemplates the nature of truth, but a definition eludes him. For something to be objectively true, he thinks, it would have to be recognized independently by others. But what has happened between him and Petra would not pass this test. The truth revealed to them is theirs alone. It is not available to other people.

★ ★ ★

Anticipation is the choicest form of pleasure. They lie side by side, touching one another, exchanging the mellifluous trifles which lovers have traded through the ages. There is no question of *thinking*, or *planning* the next few moments; only of responding to some basic atavistic drive, of moving imperceptibly from one whispered endearment to another.

He traces the contours of her soft body with the tip of his finger. He slides over her moist skin, through the sweet valley between her breasts, around the slight swell of her stomach, pausing for a brief moment in the dip of her navel. Then down, down, across the satin symmetry of her loins.

They play with each other like wet seal pups, their bodies making succulent, slipping sounds. With his tongue he caresses her and spins a silver spider's web from the threads of her wetness. The pathway to heaven pouts like the calix of a flower turned to the sun, the inner petals drenched in nectar. Her beautiful mound rises and falls as she rubs herself against his chin.

As she trembles and gasps and comes, he feels a surge of happiness and an infusion of supreme power. Her juices trickle down like a cluster of stars from the firmament. He can do anything now. He is God in one of his incarnations, spreading love and joy. Her amber thighs rear on either side like the waters parted for Moses. He rises and enters her. *He is naked, stripped of his garments.*

Eleven

The categorical imperative has always appealed to Carlo. The certainty of what we *ought* to do seems to him to rest at the very heart of morality. The concept attracts him because it provides reasoned principles of action. In the light of these principles, our own selfish hopes and wishes and desires can be examined and assessed. But these are subordinate ultimately to a higher notion of reasoned conduct. In this way the categorical imperative transcends ordinary considerations and provides us with *overriding* reasons for behaving in a moral way.

As Carlo sees it, part of the attraction of the rational way of life is the *dignity* associated with it. Dignity has always seemed to him to be a peculiarly English grace, a nobility of spirit to which he ardently aspires. It is the quality he most associates with his father. In Carlo's business which is very much concerned with profit and loss and material success, decisions are made daily on the basis of what is likely to be profitable for the company. This is of course an important consideration in running a business; but Carlo has not made it an *overriding* consideration in the larger moral scheme of things.

To the outsider the advertising world is perhaps not an obvious place for complex moral problems. But in Carlo's experience it is beset by ethical factors, which he takes a certain pride in handling. In the cases where he has been presented with a conflict of interests, or a business problem of particular complexity, he has always appealed to some impersonal notion of morality based on unconditional principles of conduct. His reward has been a sense of his own scrupulousness, a notion of his own moral integrity.

This way of thinking, however, now seems to belong to a previous existence. His professional life, and the problems associated with it, now seem impossibly remote. They are part of the world *before Petra*. It is not that he has suddenly devised a different scheme of morality, or that he regrets the old way of dealing with situations. It is much more that the old way now seems to be hopelessly inadequate. The situations he has managed at work, even the most difficult and exacting, suddenly seem to have been entirely straightforward compared to what faces him now. At this moment in his life Carlo feels confronted by a moral choice of unparalleled difficulty.

Most people behave well in the areas of their lives which are relatively uncomplicated. Other areas in which they might readily expand their goodness remain largely unexplored. There are scattered pockets of goodness all around, intimations of the human potential for virtue. When these are laudable, they are admired by others; when they are outstanding, they can even inspire others. But most people manage to avoid serious challenges in the arena of goodness. Carlo is no exception.

Although there is no shortage of definitions, goodness remains a rather vague concept. We speak nebulously about 'a good man' or 'a good woman', as if we might immediately recognize them when we see them. But those who seek to live a good life are not a homogeneous species. They can be engaged, for example, either in maximizing happiness in the world — their own and other people's; or they can be concerned with choosing the worthiest and most virtuous path. The two are not at all the same.

This is a distinction which really only achieved prominence with the advent of Christianity. For it is a central notion of the Christian ideal that the poor and meek are blessed. The converse of this is equally fundamental: *for what shall it profit a man, if he shall gain the whole world, and lose his own soul?* Carlo speaks this sentence in his head and is struck for the first time by its empty rhetoric. Of course when Jesus spoke the words they were intended to convey the wisdom that the best life materially is very different from the best life morally. But it has become a rather pious sentiment which people now express when they are being portentous. What exactly could it *mean* to gain the whole world? Or to lose one's soul for that matter? It certainly does not apply to Carlo who, if anything, has *discovered* his soul for the very first time.

The other problem with the religious concept of goodness is that it invariably involves suffering.

Goodness is when a person acts with restraint, when he directs attention away from himself. It excludes the notion of selfishness, of personal gain. But it is one thing for Carlo to act with restraint in the world of business; quite another to apply it to the most intimate part of his life.

In any case what exactly makes a good person? He tries hard to summon up a picture of a good man, but he cannot. Of course there are historical examples – Christ being the obvious one – but goodness as an idea remains elusive. Carlo decides it is most often applied to people who lead simple, unselfish, steadfast lives. And he realizes with a blinding clarity that he can no longer include his own among them. Yet he cannot think of himself as a *bad* man.

The trouble is that his dilemma is one of infinite complexity. It is not easily solved by reference to normal standards of morality. He feels more challenged, more vulnerable, than ever he has felt in his professional life. Even in his domestic world, he can recall only rare disturbances to the prevailing equilibrium. And they have certainly not entailed a great deal of pain or sacrifice.

To be regarded now as morally suspect is almost

more than Carlo can bear. Already he can sense his brothers' disapproval, the reproachful looks whenever they see him with Petra. He is beginning to understand, perhaps for the first time, that moral judgements are applied from the outside. They are imposed by people who, even if they *know* the facts, do not themselves *experience* them. The categorical imperative now seems to him to be flawed and deficient. It is quite insufficient to deal with human frailty and the outer edges of emotion. Carlo sees no point in a moral scheme which is unable to take account of the impossible tangle of human experience.

His dilemma is simply enough stated. He loves Petra. He also loves his wife. To leave his wife is out of the question. Yet to give up Petra is unthinkable. Somehow for him to survive – or at least to avoid the most abject suffering – the seemingly irreconcilable must be reconciled.

★ ★ ★

The solution, when it came, was beautifully simple. He lies in bed, Petra cradled in the crook of his arm, and the answer is just *there*, crystalline, making him think that perhaps he has dreamed it. Not dreamed it in the sense of it being ethereal or indistinct, for it is already wonderfully well-defined; but in the sense of having formulated it in the depths and peace of sleep. He moves it up and down the avenues of his mind, checking for snags or imperfections, but he finds none. He is staggered by the sheer fineness of it.

Gently, gently, he removes his arm from beneath Petra's body and raises himself on one elbow. She is beautiful in repose, the soft contours of her face relaxed and satisfied by sleep and love. He is wide awake and wanting her, as much because of the excitement of his idea as the pull of her naked body. She will be so happy when he tells her.

He marvels at the plain eroticism of the moment, so delicate yet so potent. His lips engage her dark nipple, and easing it this way and that, he stirs the woman within her. She moans sweetly, drowsily, as he urges himself into her petalled cleft. She emerges from her dream to feel the tensed muscles of his broad back under her fingers as he possesses her. Then, an urgent sob before the primal thump of his heart.

★ ★ ★

— Petra, my love, what we have between us is so wonderful. It musn't become just a memory, a thought inside your head and mine, a parenthesis in our lives. We can't let that happen. It's far too precious for that. *Let us have a child*.

She notices that his breathing is laboured. He hesitates between phrases, as if each is being fashioned and moulded before it is given voice and presented like an artefact. To be wondered at and admired.

— A child will be ours, it will belong to us, no one else. A child will sanctify our love, immortalize it, make it a living, vital thing. Our lives are circumscribed — we both know that — and we have responsibilities to others. But a child will preserve our passion, it will be a glorious celebration of our love. A *binding*.

She notes that he says *child* and not *baby*, as if to

make the idea more substantial, more determinate. A baby is too delicate, too vulnerable. They are lying side by side, so she cannot see his face, his eyes. His words hang in the air like a morning mist.

– I can't bear to think of our love as just an interlude, a brief intermezzo set apart from the real play of life. It mustn't be just something that happened between two people somewhere on the gauge of time. Love is not an ephemeral thing. Like beauty and art, it has a permanence which transcends the rigours of time. A child will be a confirmation of *us*.

She loves the timbre of his voice, solemn, majestic, seductive. It vibrates through her naked body, which adheres hotly to his. She feels quite giddy with desire, and wishes she had been awake enough earlier to come with him.

– The child will live with you and your husband. It will have two parents – only you and I will know it is *our* love-child. And it will be part of me in quite a different way from my sons. It will be my link with the past, the Italian side of me.

And I'm sure it will be a daughter, a picture of loveliness with beautiful dark eyes. She will look like you, and also my mother when she was young. And she will grow up in the sun, and run free as the air. She will be how I remember my own childhood.

She half turns and lays her hand across the parallel lines of his ribs. Compressing his thigh between hers, she begins to move rhythmically against his firm flesh. His words fill her head and travel down through her body to converge on the centre where they pile up, one on another, heightening her tension. Her senses are both within her and without, a beautiful erotic mix which builds to a momentum of its own. And is unstoppable.

− You will be a wonderful mother. You must have wanted a child more than anything in the world. And now you have the chance. The more I think about it, the more it seems there is no alternative. As an idea, it's not just inspired − it's *imperative*. A child will allow you to love in a new way, to focus all your qualities on a living person who will be part of you. It will bring fresh promise to your marriage. It will fulfil you beyond your sweetest dreams. *Petra, you will have our child, won't you?*

It is a full minute before Petra answers. She clears her throat, softly, resolutely.

'No.'

And her word clinches his heart like a nail on a cross. *It is his crucifixion.*

Twelve

Petra has a talent for common sense. Not the dull, sober variety which never falters or teeters on life's verges; but the instinctual, self-preserving kind which recognizes that the very passions which enfold us also block our vision.

She contemplates the responsibilities of love, and finds them daunting. Firstly, there is the love she feels for her husband. Petra thinks of their marriage as a vast desert, relieved by occasional watering holes and green patches where they rendezvous affectionately. It is a long term covenant, a repository of shared experience, a memory bank. It is much more a commitment than a consuming passion.

Secondly, there is her love of her career, which

stimulates and sustains her. She is respected by her colleagues, and admired by her students. Her research is not remote or esoteric, but grounded in man's struggle to make sense of the world, and as such it absorbs and satisfies her. There are opportunities for occasional amorous attachments, which also nourish. But ultimately her work provides intellectual fulfilment, which is achieved more by the orgasms of the mind than anything else.

Where does her love for Carlo fit in, if love is what it is? She turns this question over in her mind, and decides that it fits into all the recesses and excesses of her being. In the extravagance and exhilaration of it all, she has discovered something very deep in her womanhood, something which makes her rejoice in her gender. Sexual passion of the intensity she feels for Carlo unleashes in her an appetite for the rest of life, and that makes the pain of separation worthwhile. She has been on the brink of similar alliances before — though nothing quite so impassioned — and the benefits are prodigious.

Ultimately, however, they lack purity, simplicity. Part of their thrill and strength is in the fact that they are disallowed, and once there is an attempt to endorse or preserve them, they begin to fall apart. Or at least that is how she imagines it to be. She has never lingered long enough to be certain.

It is not that she considers Carlo as a passing sexual need. (In her experience there is always more to sexual need than sexual need.) But in the interests of self-preservation she has to believe that it *will* pass. The happiness she feels is a sort of giddiness, a delicious delirium, but it is, finally, a myth. And when you submit to a myth you lose the faculty of judgement. Petra has loved submitting to the myth, but life is a daily thing, something to be got through as well as romanticized.

She believes it is different for Carlo. He does not yet know what she knows. He is too rational and sensitive to survive a life of passionate chaos. His best chance of recovery is with his wife, and Petra must help him to reach that understanding. His mother's death has made him particularly vulnerable. Weakened by bereavement, he is defenceless against the soothing effects of intimacy. Sex is such a *comfort*, a healing balm, which Carlo has confounded with something more enduring and sublime. Together they have created a fantasy; a loving fantasy, but a fantasy nonetheless.

A child would be part of that fantasy. It grieves her to walk away from the possibility, which she dare not even predicate in her imagination. It is a disciplined decision, for in the most secret corner of her mind she knows that her urge to have a child is almost as basic as her urge to have sex. She is moved by the idea, but she is afraid to submit to the dream. Good sense must prevail. The cravings of her body have got her into this situation; she must rely on her head to get her out.

★ ★ ★

Carlo sits at the wooden table which, only a week ago, supported his mother's livid corpse. He looks around the room where everything is neat and ordered and completely lifeless. A week ago he predicted that without his mother the carefully constructed edifices of his life would crumble. But he could not have foreseen the manner in which this would come to pass.

Petra's answer – her chilling, deadly, unambiguous *No* – is one of those hammer blows of desolation which strike savagely and mutilate both thought and action. He is trying *not* to think, but just to *do*, to lose himself in simple practical tasks. He has telephoned his wife and told her he will be back within twenty-four hours. He has washed, changed his clothes and put most of his things in his leather bag, ready for the journey home.

And now he is cutting some bread for lunch. It is not at all fresh, but that scarcely matters. He has no appetite anyway. He is quite unconcerned as the knife slips and nicks his finger. The blood seeps from the wound and is soaked up by the bread. Carlo watches, as if observing some holy ritual. He feels entirely disconnected from what is happening. He might be a schoolboy watching a routine scientific experiment — quite interesting, but nothing really to do with *me*.

The pain of the cut is not localized, just part of the sweeping anguish which consumes him. He is glad he feels pain. Glad to be feeling something, anything. On the rare occasions when he felt miserable as a child he would try to think of something worse. If he fell and hurt his leg he would try to picture his leg being amputated. If his mother was angry with him he would try to imagine what it would be like not to have a mother. This would act as a kind of smokescreen for long enough to soften his immediate distress.

Carlo cannot imagine what kind of smokescreen could possibly help now. Except perhaps the white ants and their unrelieved darkness. Or the poor winged variety whose rare gift of flight leads cruelly to slaughter. Isn't that what has happened to him? He was given wings for only a few days, and he took to the air, soaring high, brushing the very heavens. And now, like some modern fall of Icarus, he is plunged into a sea of despair.

The coherence of things is gone. He tries to sift through the wreckage to see if anything survives intact. But he feels completely enervated, debilitated by thoughts which seem to be taking place somewhere *outside* his head. Images form and dissolve in his mind like the changing patterns of a kaleidoscope. Thought and behaviour are no longer in any kind of alignment. He is able – just – to control simple movements, but only with the greatest difficulty. There is a delay between his brain sending out instructions and his body obeying them. Everything is taking place in grotesquely slow motion.

Will he ever get back to that solid reasonable

vision which tied him to the real world? It is difficult even to remember what the real world looks like. It is ingrained in him at a deep level to think of it as a safe, ordered place. But he cannot get beyond a general, indeterminate picture. At this moment all he knows for certain is that reality has very little connection with the blood-soaked bread on the table in front of him.

When we are very young we think that there is a solution to every problem. It is only when we are older that this strikes us as naive. Perhaps he will simply have to move very gently from hour to hour, accepting what each brings. For the moment he is stuck in a cruel hiatus, a mere corridor of life, and none of it is worth a comma in history. He is overwhelmed by a sense of his own insignificance. Apart from that all he can think of is Petra: that he loves her, that she has gone, and that he feels as a consequence only half-alive.

★ ★ ★

Carlo is on his way to church not so much to bargain with God, as to ask for help. Like the closing of a crow's wing, dusk is spreading over the town. In his heart he knows that Catholicism is a humane and tolerant religion. In the half-light the piazza is a place of shadows and uncertainty. Catholicism is the only faith consistent with the moral freedom of man and his experience of the world. On the far side in front of the church a hunched figure is sweeping up the day's debris, like some dark vulture. Carlo is in a state of quiet desperation. Religion is his only hope.

He is veering madly between feeling very little and being awash with unmanageable thoughts and emotions. He has been trying to wade through the swamp of his mind in the hope of finding something firm to hold on to. But all attempts are impeded by a piercing nostalgia for the comfort and safety of his childhood. He remembers the convent, with its shining floors, its smell of beeswax, the rythmic rituals, the trading in certainties. He thinks of the sweet devotion of Sister Ignatia, her simplicity of faith. What would she think of him now?

Are the faithful good because they believe? Or do they believe because they are good? Is unbelief unworthy? Is faith innately virtuous? The questions flood Carlo's mind, but the answers elude him. He wants to believe that faith must somehow be consonant with reason, but reason must surely also be a gift from God. It is all so terribly complicated.

What we learn by rote as children is stored in the memory and never forgotten. In the convent there was a great deal of reciting out loud and learning by heart. It was part of the certainty, the atmosphere of absolute conviction. Knowing what the words meant seemed not to matter. What mattered was being able to repeat them correctly without faltering. Most of what the children chanted was from the Catechism, but there were other maxims of mysterious provenance. As Carlo enters the Madonna del Rosario he remembers Sister Ignatia's favourite: *The perpetual play of good and evil is enacted on the human stage through the experience of Death, Suffering, Sin and Grace.* The words are etched on his memory as plainly as Sister Ignatia chalked them on the blackboard. *Death, Suffering, Sin and Grace.* Can he have acted out the whole gamut of human drama since he last set foot in the church, less than a week ago? Does God have a sense of humour? The comic absurdity does not escape Carlo, but he experiences it as another level of hopelessness.

Death and Suffering are clear enough. It is not only the death of his mother, but the loss of Petra. Without a child their love affair is over. Dead. As dead as their unbegotten child. *Sin and Grace* are more problematic. Was it really a sin to make love to Petra? If so, sin and grace are sisters under the skin, for in his passion for Petra he had felt nearer to God than ever before.

Carlo moves unsteadily up the aisle and makes the sign of the cross before turning into the left transept. It is lit only by the flicker of nearly-spent candles. Here he falls to his knees in front of the painting of the Madonna and cradles his face in his hands. It is not as if he has been *casually* unfaithful. What happened might just as easily never have happened. He did not seek it. It was just *there*, and he embraced it as he might delight in a work of fine art. He is enlarged and uplifted by his knowledge of Petra as he might be by a beautiful painting.

He is aware that this sounds like special pleading, but the truth of the analogy is in his own experience of both. If one act is deemed 'sinful' and the other not, that is only because sinfulness is insinuated in the fleshliness. But that is a judgement imposed by others from outside, not an empirical truth. How could it be *God's* judgement? In His omniscience He must have known that the Fall of Man would occur. That is an essential part of His creation, the arrangement He made for us. Man sins only because he has been granted free will. And free will is truly free only in the context of the full range of human experience. That includes Petra and Flora, and lovers and sinners everywhere. This would be true even in a Godless world, because of the nature of life and death. Men and women have seemingly acquired great power and knowledge, but in the context of their brief lifespan all seems futile and transient. Man is doomed, whether by God's design or by natural causes.

However, man is condemned more by his fellow man than by God, for the concept of redemption is inseparable from the Fall of Man. If man sins he has to have the possibility of forgiveness from a merciful God. Otherwise the whole system breaks down and becomes meaningless. In the meantime sin continues to be portrayed as human weakness; invariably by those who cannot, *will not*, see it also as a source of great spiritual strength. Despite his present anguish, Carlo knows that he has been elevated by it, extended by it, that he understands the human condition better because of it. It is a surrendering to the unknown.

The judgement of men is flawed and imperfect, like men themselves. We are all implicated in sin, whether it be infidelity or anything else. And those who preach and moralize are perhaps in particular danger because of their own limitations, their lack of compassion, their ignorance of human affairs.

Carlo is addressing this torrent of thoughts to the Madonna. Some of them are spoken aloud, others choked back by the remains of self-control. He is trapped in a maze of conflicting feelings and has a sharp pain in his head. He also feels a trembling in his limbs, not unlike the sensation that day on the hillside. He scrutinizes the perfect features of the *Mater Dolorosa*, hoping for comfort but finding none. She is the person in whom all contradictions are supposedly reconciled. But the double ideal she represents is unachievable by ordinary mortals. She is set apart by God from the human race, denied the quintessential part of human experience. She is a myth created by man and by God. She is beautiful and good and perfect, but ultimately she has no moral relevance for humanity.

Carlo feels the sting of his sad salt tears, and his vision blurs. He remembers how the Madonna's tears helped him in the hour of his bereavement. For an instant he thinks he sees Petra's face overlaid on the painting, like a negative doubly exposed. His spirits lift momentarily, but in another instant she is gone. It is all an illusion. And with her, everything is gone. All faith, all hope, all charity. Gone, gone, gone. *It is a giving up of the spirit.*

Thirteen

Carlo wakes to the cool blue light of his last morning in Italy. He lies very still to check on his state of mind, and is surprised and relieved to be feeling so *well*. The shutters are already open as they have been all night, and the single curtain sighs softly on the tiled floor. He listens to the morning sounds – bristle on stone stairways, the splash of water on plants, and the freshness of exchanged greetings. He moves to the window from where he can see that the new day is already well underway.

Streamers of washing are stretched between balconies, and bright cushions are in place on the hard iron chairs outside the cafés. A little to the right Carlo sees a brisk young waiter, whistling tunelessly and brushing a profusion of petals from the white tables. The petals have fallen from the riotous blue and white climber cascading down the south-facing wall of the café. Carlo recognizes it as the passion flower, *Passiflora*, the name given to it by Spanish priests who saw in the flowers the symbols of Christ's passion.

He knows all this from his own dear Flora – so named by her parents after the goddess of flowers – whose devotion to gardening is second only to her family commitments. He remembers her pride when her own carefully nurtured passion flower had first blossomed, now many summers ago. She had taken Carlo to the most sheltered spot in her beloved garden and shown him the white and blue blooms, as a mother might show off her baby's first tooth. There she had explained to him, in the manner of a teacher in love with her subject, that the ten white petals of each flower represented Christ's disciples, minus Judas and Peter, while the ring of fine blue filaments symbolized the crown of thorns. In the centre the three stigmas were the crosses of Christ and the thieves, and the yellowish stains depicted the wounds. The last thing she told him was that each flower blooms only for one day before it withers and dies. He remembers this detail particularly, because he had expected her to be sad, and she had surprised him by being utterly matter-of-fact. He envies Flora her sensible approach to life, her complete acceptance of the fact that things, even the most beautiful things, wither and die.

Sensible is a word often applied to Flora, not just by Carlo, but by her own mother and friends. Carlo regrets the rather disparaging overtones of the English word which, perversely, has nothing at all to do with sensibility. Somehow she deserves a better word, to take account of her capacity to feel.

He is pleased now to be thinking of Flora. He closes his eyes, half expecting her to disappear as he does so, but her image stays, and he feels a happy relief. He opens his eyes in time to see the waiter sweep the dead passion flowers into a neat little pile. Nothing beautiful, he thinks, even if it dies, is ever worthless, to no avail. This has everything to do with faith, and nothing to do with reason. Somewhere in the distance beyond the petals Carlo recognizes the faintest glimmer of recovery.

★ ★ ★

Carlo waits for the train to arrive at the small picturesque station bedecked in roses and trailing pelargoniums. In a few minutes his visit will move from the present, which has to be lived through, to the past which will then be over, and no more than a memory. In his brothers' farewells he detects a kind of quiet confidence, as if they are on the point of solving a problem. They embrace tightly, but somehow uneasily. There is no time to explain anything, and no point.

As the train pulls into the station, Carlo gives them a final smile, half valedictory, half apologetic, before he disappears inside the compartment. From his window seat he looks along the platform where assorted boxes of produce are being loaded onto the train and a porter is piling cases onto a trolley.

Amidst the busyness Carlo's eyes light on a pretty young girl, her head turning this way and that, waiting expectantly for someone. The early sun is behind her, rendering her thin cotton dress translucent. She runs her hand through her dark hair, and Carlo is immediately reminded of Petra. After a moment or two her face becomes radiant with the happiness of recognition. She runs, arms outstretched, to greet an older man, who hugs her and kisses her warmly. They are happy together. Carlo feels both the awkwardness and tenderness occasioned by watching other people's intimacy. The couple begin to walk away, arm in arm, their heads flung back in laughing contentment, and at that moment Carlo realizes with something akin to shock that they are not lovers, but father and daughter.

As the train pulls slowly out of the station Carlo is greatly moved by the receding image of what might have been. And what cannot now be. But at the same time, from out of the wistful wreckage, a kind of resignation emerges, like lotus petals peeping above the murkiness of a pond. *He is taken down from the cross.*

Fourteen

The shock is in the familiar. The stack of beautifully ironed laundry, the fragrance of Flora's perfume, the unvarying throb of the children's music coming from upstairs. Cookery books, fresh cut flowers, domesticity. Everything seems slightly exaggerated, larger than normal, as if seen through a magnifying lens.

He knows that Flora is no different, but her perfectly ordinary movements, such as pouring tea from the pot, or slipping her heels out of her shoes, seem quite exceptional. He feels himself being pulled and nudged, eased gently into the safe anchorage of household and family. Before long it is the other world which seems strange and perilous.

* * *

To tell or not to tell: the tension between these two simple choices has the power to wreck lives. He knows that even in his own previously sheltered existence there have certainly been times when he would much rather not have known the details of some hideously intimate scene between individuals, particularly those closest to him. Ignorance often protects, and reduces suffering.

He also knows that despite Flora's directness — not harsh, just honest — there is an element of concealment, a degree of privacy which is common to most middle-class Englishwomen. Some subjects are simply not up for discussion, being either too painful or too distasteful.

In contrast to the great emotional sweep of the other world, Carlo and Flora operate within neat, well-defined precincts. Flora is happy in her own skin. Her natural desires for self-fulfilment are perfectly realized in house and husband, children and garden. She brings the same warm enthusiasm to looking after her family as she does to tender plants in her greenhouse. She belongs to the last generation of women who can still feel that they lead useful lives without having to have an outside job. She has quite escaped the scourge of feminism and hence the guilt associated with its practical application. All the corners of her life are filled with a busyness and contentment. This might be a limitation in some women; in Flora it is a clever accomplishment.

Carlo turns over these qualities in his mind, as if handling fine china. The roots of their relationship lie very deep, perhaps too deep to be disturbed. But he knows that she is compassionate and forgiving, and commendably stoical when required. Their marriage, he thinks, would almost certainly survive the telling, though the possibility for distress in almost limitless. He cannot bear to hurt her and make her feel betrayed.

And yet the consequences of *not* telling are paved with guilt and uncertainty.

★ ★ ★

She has made a special meal for him – consommé, followed by duck in orange and port sauce. The claret is decanted and chambréd. She is wearing a fine silk scarf, a touch of elegance over her everyday cotton shirt. She is cheerful and affectionate, pleased to see him. He feels welcome, *wanted*. She serves up the soup, chatting happily all the while, bringing him up to date with all that has happened in his absence. He sits opposite her like a man sitting at the edge of the sea, letting each incoming wave wash over him.

— *Flora, we must talk about what happened in Italy.*

— *Yes, I want to hear all about it when you're ready.*

— *Darling, it was all so strange. A time quite unrelated to my life here, a time set apart. I felt quite isolated.*

— *I suppose I really should have come with you. You shouldn't have had to go through all that on your own.*

— *There was no need for you to come. I actually wanted to be on my own . . . only . . .*

— *It must have brought back so many memories — the place, your brothers, old friends, meeting people.*

— *I did meet people, yes. That's what I wanted to talk to you about really. There was someone, a woman who turned up at the funeral . . .*

— *A friend of the family?*

— *Yes, in a way. I saw her after the funeral too. She became quite special to me . . .*

— *I'm glad. Bereavement is such an awful shock. You need someone to lean on. I remember how I felt when my father died. I needed comfort then too.*

— *Flora, I want you to know . . .*

— *I do know, darling. Death is a terrible business, and it will take you a long time to get over it. But you will get over it. It's just a question of time . . .*

There is a space around her which seems inviolable. His attempts to tell her move like eddies against the main current of her mysterious composure. The telephone rings. She leaves the room to answer it, kissing his cheek as she goes, taking with her partial visions of truth.

On the chair behind him is a schoolbook, an A-level text of T S Eliot's *Four Quartets*. Carlo opens it idly and leafs through the pages. A marker is placed at the fourth quartet, *Little Gidding* which, it is explained, is a 17th century manor where a religious community followed a rule of private devotion and study. Carlo skims the poem till his eyes rest on the three lines highlighted in blue pen by his son:

> *And the end of all our exploring*
> *Will be to arrive where we started*
> *And know the place for the first time.*

The words swish round his head like the sound of the sea in a dream. A faint image of Petra hovers in front of his eyes. He adjusts his breathing and waits for it to go. Everything which might have been is no more. It is over. *Buried*.

★ ★ ★

The September sky is an undecided mixture of powdery blue and white. In her office on the fourth floor of a modern building at the University of Naples, Petra is sitting in an armchair surrounded by a pile of books and an open notepad. Her eyes are closed, and her head, which feels heavy, is resting on the back of the chair. It is uncomfortably hot for September. She undoes the first few buttons of her blue silk shirt. A trickle of sweat runs between her full breasts. She spreads her hands over the slight swell of her belly. Her heart is full of love and longing, which makes her feel quite faint. Deep inside her, there is the first flutter of life, like a crocus pushing through snow.